This is to acknowledge my appreciation
for the immense encouragement and inspiration given to
me by my wife Mithu and my daughter Shahzeen.
It was their persistence that I share my stories with the
world that made this book possible.
Thank you, you two.

THE CORE ESSENCE

TALES FROM THE HEART

RAVI SHIVDASANI

INDIA • SINGAPORE • MALAYSIA

ISBN 979-8-89133-998-9

TABLE OF CONTENTS

NOTE TO THE READER

This book is all about experiences through the journey of life; its mottled and varied emotions, some good times and some bad times. Once I started writing this book, it was like I was driven to share these stories with the world and was left with a feeling of pensive happiness and upliftment. I hope you will also feel as I did, dear reader, when you finish reading my short stories.

ACKNOWLEDGEMENTS

Obviously, the first thank you is to my family and friends, who literally egged me on to get these stories published. It was their unfailing support and reaction to my stories that ensured that I was on the right path. In particular, I would like to thank Malini, who helped me with the editing, and Kalyan, who helped me reach out to a select few publishers.

And last but not least, the various strangers I met who entrusted me with their tales and moved me to pen them down for a wider audience. If it wasn't for them, this book would never have happened.

GUEST IN MY OWN HOUSE

Jagdish felt a jolt that shook him out of his deep slumber. 'The cruise liner must have docked at the port,' he thought to himself. He bounded out of bed, quickly wore his nightgown, slipped on his slippers, and sped up to the deck.

His childhood mate Ravi was already standing by the ship's railings, looking at the city, and, as Jagdish joined Ravi in a hug, they both got teary-eyed as they silently gazed upon what had once been the centre of their existence. Their beloved city, the city of their childhood—Karachi.

It seemed that eons had passed in what had only been just over a year. Jagdish remembered that evening at the old Parsee Café, when Jadish, Ravi, Saleem, and Akbar had mused about the future.

The four young men had been the best of friends since the fifth grade. The foursome, a popular lot, were known as Comedy Central, and had only just recently graduated with top-of-the-class performances from Karachi University, doing their parents proud. Over the years, the boys' parents too had developed a strong bond, and the four families would meet often to celebrate happy occasions. Jagdish and Saleem had graduated with a degree in law and Ravi and Akbar had degrees in finance and accounts.

The conversation at Parsee Café had centred around the rumours that India was to be broken apart into two countries, India and Pakistan, during the forthcoming pull-out by the British Empire on Independence Day. Ravi had voiced the opinion that he was doubtful about whether Hindus would be welcome in Muslim Pakistan. The new country was going to be called the Islamic Republic of Pakistan. 'How can you have a country that is defined by religion? Is the state not supposed to be truncated from religion in a functioning democracy? Was that not the basic tenet of a democracy as defined by the Ancient Greeks?'

The other three strongly disagreed with Ravi. Jagdish pointed out that the part of India that was being charted out as Pakistan consisted predominantly of Muslims influenced by Sufism. 'So this is going to be a very tolerant, all-embracing Muslim state that will encourage and respect all religions.'

'We all have lived in complete harmony for decades. Look at our four families—the perfect example. Nothing will change,' Akbar argued vehemently.

Saleem watched the expressions flitting over Ravi's face, then reached out and clasped Ravi's forearm. 'Say what is on your mind, Ravi,' Saleem said quietly. 'Say it aloud.'

Ravi then voiced the unthinkable as three heads swung to look at Ravi in shocked silence. 'Maybe we Hindus should consider relocating to India' Ravi said softly. Saleem and Akbar jumped up from their chairs and held Ravi in a bear hug as Jagdish watched the three in pensive silence.

Karachi in July was swelteringly hot. The lads met every day, as was the norm, and over innumerable cups of masala chai and delicious bun maskas served by Rustomjee, the owner of Parsee Café, the four contemplated what the future held for them. Pakistan would be faced with innumerable challenges, but with all four communities working together, contributing their specific skills to the new state, the future looked ever so bright. Akbar enthusiastically said, 'We will create a new land together, the land of the pure … Pakistan.' All four raised their tea cups with a resounding cheer.

But, for Jagdish and Ravi, fate had other plans. It was 9 pm of July 20th. Parts of Karachi were breaking out into riots and street fighting. Hindu families were scared for their safety. The doorbell at Jagdish's house on Bunder Road Extension chimed urgently. Jagdish and his father ran to the main gate of the villa.

'Who is it?' Jagdish asked.

'It is Abba and me,' Akbar replied. 'Open the door quickly.'

Jagdish opened the door. Akbar and his father Saifuddin entered and hastily shut the door behind them. Saifuddin turned to Ravi's dad Nitin and said, 'Nitin, the news is not good. I have heard there are going to be riots in Bunder Road Extension tonight and mobs will be attacking Hindu families. You, Savitri, the girls, and Jagdish must move to my house immediately. Pack what little you can, only essentials, and come as fast as possible. I am waiting in the car. As we speak, Saleem and Moinuddin are collecting Ravi, Ram, and Pushpa and will take them to their house. Please make haste, my friend.' Saifuddin gently laid his hand on Nitin's shoulder before stepping out of the villa to wait in the car. Akbar followed Nitin and Jagdish into the villa.

The family packed their dearest belongings and quickly got into Saifuddin's car with Jadish and Akbar loading the luggage into the boot and just as Jagdish stepped into the car he looked back at the house of his childhood as if to say 'see you soon', little realizing how swiftly fate was going to play its part in this theatre of the absurd.

The next morning, news of the Bunder Road Massacre filtered through. Human bestiality at its worst. As Akbar and Jagdish stepped into the breakfast room, the scene that unfolded before them was grim. The ladies were all at the dining table, pretending to keep themselves busy with serving breakfast, and, as Akbar's mother Nafeesa leaned forward to hug Savitri, Savitri broke down crying. Jagdish's sisters looked at him helplessly as he moved forward quickly to hold them. The two fathers were sitting on the sofa talking to each other in hushed tones. Seeing the two boys, they beckoned them closer.

Nitin said to them, 'Saifuddin is advising us to leave for Bombay tonight. We will stay with Uncle Bhagat there.

Let all this quieten down and we will return to Karachi later. Ravi and his parents will also join us on the flight to Bombay. They, too, have relatives in Bombay. Just thank God and our dear friends that we are alive and safe.' He gratefully clasped Saifuddin's hand.

At seven p.m. that night, they drove to the airport. Ravi and his parents joined them. The airport was crowded with terrified people trying to find their way out of this hell that Karachi had become for Hindus. The four families hugged each other and the four boys went into a group hug. No words were spoken, but there was not a single dry eye amongst them.

As the departees were walking towards the plane, Ravi witnessed a scene that haunted him for the rest of his life. A distraught young woman holding a two-year-old child fell at Savitri's feet and begged her to take her child to safety—to India. The security personnel held the young lady back as Nitin and Jagdish helped a visibly shaken and deeply disturbed Savitri onto the plane, and as the plane taxied for take-off, there was a deep sigh of relief from all of them, tinged with a palpable feeling of a deep loss.

Uncle Bhagat was at the airport to greet them and was delighted to have his brother and family safe with him in Bombay. Uncle Bhagat was a dry fruit trader and ran an extremely successful business. He lived in an eight-bedroom villa in Bombay's tony Malabar Hill, was married to Tenaaz, a Parsi, and had one child, Rohit. Tenaaz and Rohit were at the entrance to the villa to greet their Karachi cousins and Jagdish and family quickly settled into their new, comfortable surroundings.

The next month was spent getting to know Bombay better. Ravi and his family were staying at Altamount Road, which was a stone's throw from Malabar Hill. The two lads met every evening and tried creating a zone of comfort on the gorgeous Café Naaz terrace overlooking Marine Drive. Weekends were about getting to know the City better. Both families had become members of the Willingdon Club and the lads often played tennis at the Club. Being friendly and gregarious by nature, they soon had a wide circle of friends and were often invited for dinner at the homes of their many new acquaintances. But every conversation at Café Naaz veered towards the latest update from Akbar and Saleem. It was as if a part of them was missing and, although they did not explicitly express it, both of them felt incomplete.

The four families were constantly in touch with each other on the phone and through weekly letters. There had been equally horrifying acts committed in Bombay against Muslims, but, one month down the line, things had settled down both in Bombay and Karachi.

Uncle Bhagat was insisting that Nitin and Jagdish join him as partners to expand his business. After much persuasion, Nitin agreed, and both father and son started attending the office to understand and master the ropes of the dry fruit business. A corollary to that was that Jagdish and family were going to make Bombay their home. Nitin wanted to move out, but Jagdish and Tenaaz would have none of that. So, two months into his move to India, Jagdish and his family had metamorphised into a joint family and adopted a new city, a new business—a completely new life.

Ravi's family too had undergone a change. They had moved out to a two-bedroom flat in Altamount Road. Ravi's father had taken up an assignment with Bombay Port Trust and Ravi had joined Price Waterhouse & Co as an articled clerk, experience he required to become a chartered accountant.

Bombay was an attractive city bustling with new opportunities, new friends, new places to visit, and a feeling of belonging; but when they spoke about it, they all expressed a deep longing for Karachi.

It was July 1948. Uncle Bhagat was in the conference room at the office. He called for Jagdish. 'Jagdish, we have a new supplier in Beirut and Karachi. I want you to travel by liner to both places. Check out the suppliers, their quality of product, etc. You also need a break, that's why I am suggesting a cruise liner. If you want to take Ravi with you, I will bear the charges. Nitin also approves of the trip.'

The passports were prepared and the visas obtained, and both friends were super excited to leave. The cruise liner sailed out of Bombay port on August 30 and headed towards Karachi, their first port of call.

Upon their arrival, the boys quickly showered, changed, disembarked from the ship, cleared customs and port immigration, and stepped out into Karachi to a rambunctious welcome. Akbar and Saleem rushed forward to greet them, and there followed at least 15 minutes of hugging and back-slapping and tears. The four of them were meeting after slightly more than a year. They were all bunking at Akbar's place so that they could savour every minute of being together.

Rustomjee's was their first port of call the next morning. As soon as they entered the café, Rustomjee rushed out with a roar of sheer delight and loudly proclaimed, 'Free bun maskas and masala chai for all.' The four boys settled in and the conversation was fast and furious. Lots of laughter, with regulars of Rustomjee's walking up to them and sharing their happiness on seeing the four of them together again.

Saleem was the first one to bring up the issue. Jagdish's old house had been acquired by the Pakistani state under the statute of eminent domains and handed over to a Muslim family that had fled the Bombay riots and made Karachi their home.

'Do you want to see your old house, Jagdish? We can visit. The new owners are Abba's clients, and I can ask them,' Saleem said.

Jagdish thought for a minute and nonchalantly said, 'Ya, sure.' Meanwhile, he thought to himself, 'Maybe this will give me closure.'

As they turned into the lane that housed the villa, Jagdish steeled himself for the onslaught of emotions. They rang the doorbell, and the door was opened by a middle-aged man who thrust his hand out and said, 'Hi. I am Iqbal, please do come in.'

As Jagdish walked down the garden path to the villa, he just had a feeling of deep emptiness. A middle-aged woman opened the door to the villa and was introduced as Jamila, Iqbal's wife. The house was exactly as it had when they had left it a year ago. Only some pictures on the walls had been changed.

Looking at Jagdish's shocked expression, Jamila said, 'We liked it as it was and swore not to change anything in the hope that the Hindu family who was given our house in Bombay would not change anything.'

Jagdish asked whether he could see the bedrooms upstairs, especially his room.

Jamila looked for approval at Iqbal, who quietly nodded his head and said, 'Follow me.'

Once Jagdish entered his old room, the tears would not stop. Saleem, who had entered the villa with Jagdish, held him tightly and looked apologetically at Iqbal, who lowered his head in sympathy.

Jagdish managed to get a grip on himself, and the three of them headed down.

Jamila was waiting for them in the living room. 'I know this must be very difficult for you. I empathise with you completely,' she condoled.

Jagdish folded his hands wordlessly and headed towards the main door.

Jamila then addressed Saleem. 'We have a custom that no guest leaves our house without eating a snack and drinking some sherbet. May I bring you some?'

Jagdish was at the door when he seemed to freeze. He turned around, and with his hands folded in a namaste, said, 'Thank you. But I am just not used to being a guest in my own house.' He added, 'Please forgive me.'

Then he stepped out of his childhood for the last time.

ALL THINGS MUST PASS

Eshan looked at the guest list he was compiling. The Class of '72 school reunion party that he was throwing at his palatial farmhouse in Panvel was scheduled for the end of March. He was excited. There were some old mates he had not met in 50 years. They would all be hitting 65 by now. This was to be a boys-only event—no spouses to dilute the concentrated energy of catching up, using foul language, and of course serious drinking.

Eshan had planned the event to the minutest detail. He had reserved 39 rooms in the nearby Radisson Blu in Panvel. Check-in time was noon on Sunday, March 31. Ten luxury sedans had been reserved for the day to transport the guests to his farm at seven p.m. in a cavalcade of boisterous heartiness. The catering was being handled by the hotel, and Swati, the svelte and stylish marketing head of the hotel, had promised him a memorable, stylish, delicious, alcohol-laden, fun-filled evening. The Rockies, a famous band from Mumbai, would be belting out retro music and Swati, as the hostess of the evening, had designed games and quizzes that the guests could participate in. There was even a school quiz, with questions on nostalgic school events that the 40 would have to compete to remember to win a hamper.

Eshan reviewed his guest list once again. There were only 39 names on the list. He had not written in Nathan as a guest. Nathan Riberio, his best friend, his dearest fiend, his confidante, his compatriot in the escapades of youth and life.

Eshan had not been in touch with Nathan for nigh on 30 years. They had been inseparable through school and college, having both enrolled in IIT Bombay together. After college, they rented a two-BHK apartment together in Colaba and took up jobs with offices in Nariman Point. They had a single car that they both shared to and from work. The friends they individually made at work soon became common friends. To everybody that knew them, they were 'bros'—brothers in the truest sense of the word.

Eshan loved Mumbai. Hanging out at Geoffrey's Bar after work, walking down Marine Drive in the rain, and dancing the night away at The Cellar were euphoric experiences. The old British Raj architectural grandeur juxtaposed with the high-rise offices and residences gave the city character and style. The fabulous sunsets over the Arabian Sea were spectacular and soul-fulfilling. But, above all, the hearty joie de vivre of the people made the city a vibrant and scintillating place. Mumbai had a vibe, a zing, and a zest to it, a dazzle and an innate sense of beauty. 'Mumbai meri jaan,' Eshan often said aloud to himself.

And of course there was Punita, the ultimate reason Eshan could not dream of living anywhere else. Punita literally breezed into Eshaan's life at Starbucks. Eshan was walking out of the cafe and had stepped aside to make way for a very beautiful girl who walked in giving him a shy smile. It was that smile that slew him. He then saw her in the office the next day. She was Rohit's sister. Rohit was working on Eshan's team on a new refurbishment project in Fort. From that time on, there was no looking back. After a few candlelight dinners and some very satisfying lovemaking over a weekend in Alibaug, Eshan and Punita stepped forward as a couple to the rest of the world.

Obviously, Nathan was the first person who was introduced to Punita by Eshan, and the two of them seemed to get along fabulously well. Punita would very often spend the weekend at the boys' bachelor pad and soon the three of them were a team—Eshan, his girlfriend Punita, and his bro Nathan.

Eshan and Punita had been dating for two years. It was a weekend and Eshan had to fly to Delhi for a meeting with Anand a very important client who wanted to redesign his retail outlet of shoes and clothes; his speciality being designer tennis shoes. Eshan had called Punita and told her he would be out for the weekend and would call her on Sunday as soon as he got home as he dashed to the airport on Friday night and managed to just about board the Delhi flight.

The next day had been packed with meetings and, after a great dinner at Bukhara with his very satisfied client, Eshan had headed for his hotel in the limousine.

His thoughts had turned to Punita, and he had felt a great urge of wanting to be with her. He had looked at his watch; if he were quick enough, he could make the night flight to Mumbai. He would rush home and call Punita, go pick her up so that they could spend a lazy and love-filled Sunday together.

Eshan had landed in Mumbai at eleven p.m. and opened the door to step into the apartment. The lights were off in the hall but he could see the light seeping through under Nathan's door. Nathan was awake. Eshan had opened the door, and his world stopped still as he saw his 'bro' and girlfriend in bed, completely nude and in the middle of a passionate interlude. As they sprang apart, the three pairs of eyes had locked in, and Punita and Nathan had seen shock, bewilderment, disgust, and horror flit across Eshan's face. Nothing was said, no words were spoken, and Eshan had left the apartment.

From that day on, Eshan had never spoken to or seen either Punita or Nathan. He had changed jobs, taking up an assignment in Delhi with Anand. This betrayal had so deeply affected his being that Eshan had never married or allowed another being to penetrate the wall that he built around himself. Oh yes, there were many girlfriends, but all of them had walked away because, other than physical intimacy, Eshan had nothing to offer them.

'No, I will not invite Nathan, I am not ready,' Eshan thought to himself as he proceeded to send out the 39invitations.

The next few weeks flew by in a blur of activity. Confirmation emails poured in from all the guests. The hotel bookings were confirmed by all 38 guests. About a week before the party, Nathan received a call from Sudheer, an old school friend of both Nathan's and Eshan's.

'A few of us were dining at the Gym yesterday and were discussing the party next week,' Sudheer said. 'We have all seen the full guest list, Eshan. Nathan is the only one missing. Isn't it time to forgive and forget? And with all of us around, you can take it forward to the level you want it to, without any histrionics. Just think about it.'

Eshan paused before replying. Pretending to pass it off jocularly, he said with a chuckle, 'No, man, I am still jealous of him! Let it be for now. Looking forward to seeing you next week, Sudheer, I promise you the time of your life.'

It was the day of the party. The Panvel farmhouse was being decorated. The caterers had arrived at four p.m. and were setting up four large, circular tables with sparkling white tablecloth covers and chairs with white tie backs. The stage was being set and the sound system was being checked.

Around six that evening, when the doorbell rang, Eshan was busy getting things ready for the evening's party. Wondering who had turned up so early, he grumpily went to the door.

It was Nathan.

'I'm here to help you,' he said with a smile. 'How much can you possibly do all by yourself?' Extending a single rose that had a long, slender stalk, he bowed dramatically. 'Congratulations. For now, you could stop being jealous," he sneered.

Eshan knew that the emphatic 'all by yourself' was hardly intentional, but it bothered him.

'I know I am not invited, but please let me in. We need to talk,' Nathan said beseechingly.

Eshan just left the door ajar, turned his back on Nathan, and walked into the study. Nathan shut the main door, stepped into the study, and closed the study door. Then, addressing Eshan's back, he said, 'There is nothing I can say other than that what I did was dastardly, selfish, and unforgiveable. What both Punita and I did was meaningless and in a drunken stupor. We destroyed all our three lives. Punita and I have never met or spoken to each other since that day. I have missed our friendship for 40 years, my brother, and have suffered deeply without you. I miss you deeply. I have not had the courage to contact you and meet you because I don't know how to face you. That changed yesterday. I received a call from a young man, Aakash. His mother, Punita, had passed away last month and had left a letter for one Eshan. Aakash had contacted Rohit, whom I occasionally bump into at the Gym. Rohit tracked me down, and I promised to get the letter to you. So, here is the letter, Eshan. I am leaving it on the table.' After a pause, Nathan said in a whisper, 'Eshan, please, please forgive me before it is too late for us, I beg you.' He then turned around and, as he opened the study door to step out, he added, 'I have always loved you, my one and only bro.' He walked out of the study, shutting the door behind him.

Eshan stood stock-still, then slowly turned around, and, with a shaking hand, picked up the sealed envelope on the table. The envelope was addressed to him. There was a letter inside penned in Punita's distinctive classical style. It had only three lines:

My one and only love,

Please forgive me.

I have always loved only you.

Eshan could not hold back the upsurge of emotions that racked his body and he broke down, sobbing uncontrollably. With her passing words, Punita had washed away all the pain that he had bottled up over the last 40 years. He felt sadness and despair over the lost time, but, at the same time, he felt full of love and he let that overwhelm his being. 'Nathan, where is Nathan?' he thought to himself as he dashed out of the study.

Nathan was crouched outside the main door, crying quietly. Eshan ran to him and hugged him. No words were spoken, but they both new that the dark cloud was passing and that the sun was soon going to shine through.

'We better get ready, the guests will be arriving soon,' Eshan told Nathan as they headed back into the house.

The party was a huge success, and as Eshan and Nathan welcomed each guest at the door, they all hugged them both with a delighted chuckle. The 'brothers' were together, once again.

Sudheer finally put it all together. As he ended the toast to Eshan for hosting the reunion dinner, he walked to where Eshan and Nathan were standing and hugged them warmly, quietly saying, 'All things must pass.' The guests whopped out their appreciation in raucous applause.

DEALING WITH THE PLAGUE

We had reached a kind of stasis in dealing with the plague. Sure, we could not go out to a restaurant, or to the gym, or even attend a gathering of over six people, but we had taught ourselves to accept the situation as our current reality and deal with it. But that did not satisfy the plague.

The plague wanted more. As it ravaged the land for the second time like a tsunami, it left a trail of dead bodies in its wake. People were now petrified of stepping out of their homes and were fearful of even the simplest of interactions with anybody who was not a family member. Added to that, with the modern tools of social communication available, the horrendous and horrifying scenes of people dying unaided, without hospitalisation, under open skies, that were being transmitted in real time from mobile phone to mobile phone compounded the mounting fear and panic amongst the populace. This was not the world we had wanted for ourselves.

'How on earth are we supposed to deal with all this?' Suresh said aloud to himself. Suresh was 65 years old and had retired at the age of 60. He had built a life around attending the theatre and concerts, dining at restaurants, meeting with friends, and travelling. Now, due to a cruel stroke of fate, all of that had become impossible. Given his age and his multiple co-morbidities, Suresh needed to take extra care and had been confined to the four walls of his apartment. Suresh's wife Sujata and children were extra vigilant with him and did not allow him any interactions other than with members of his own family. A jail sentence if there ever was one.

Suresh looked morosely into the full-length mirror facing him. He saw a grey-haired, balding man with a surprisingly youthful face and the promise of a shy smile. A good-looking elderly gentleman with a pensive expression. 'Somewhere in all this, there is a message for me,' Suresh thought to himself. 'I think we all want to feel relevant and that's the flaw in the focus we make for ourselves. It is linked to the ego. Maybe I need to let go of that. But that's the whole issue. Assume I live for 20 years more, can I cope with not feeling relevant for that long?' The plague had really wreaked havoc on the standard, acceptable modes of traversing the journey of life.

Sujata walked into the room at that very moment. Kissing Suresh on his forehead, she joked lovingly, 'You are yet very hot, my dear hubby, but stop admiring yourself. Now, please, can we attend to our morning chores?' Sujata went through the list of payments that Suresh had to make for goods and services that they had availed of. 'Oh yes, and we have to send a letter to the society about the leakages in the kitchen,' she added. 'Now I had better rush off and attend to organising lunch.'

As he watched her leave the room, Suresh felt a rush of deep love for his wife. She was the light of his life. She brought laughter, togetherness, and a sense of belonging into his being. With her, he felt understood and appreciated. At a certain level, he also envied her. Sujata was deeply spiritual. Her mornings were devoted to prayer and organising the kitchen for the day. Afternoon was siesta time from two p.m. to four p.m. Evenings were devoted to prayer and watching serials on television. Then a glass of red wine, followed by dinner. Sujata slept at eleven p.m. every day and was up by seven a.m. in the morning. She was a very gregarious person but was quite content with interacting only with her family.

'Darling,' as she so often said, 'I get my relevance within the house. Being the sole breadwinner, you have always experienced your relevance outside the house. I completely understand what you are going through. Give it time, you will find the solution to the upheavals within you.' Strangely, that always made Suresh feel calm for a while, and it was followed by a surge of gratefulness for having Sujata by his side.

Mimi, his youngest child, bounded into the room. 'Dad, talk to me, I am getting bored.' All the three kids were working from home. The elder two, Rajesh and Sushmita, were married and lived in their own homes. Mimi, the naughtiest of the three, was a bundle of energy; very intelligent and a real spitfire. She worked as a PR consultant with ASDA. 'I have 15 minutes between Zoom calls. How has your day been so far?'

Suresh thought a bit and then decided to share his feelings of irrelevance with his youngest. Mimi listened to her Dad patiently until he had finished and then jumped into his lap, gave him a kiss on his cheek, and said in her inimitable style, 'Pops, chill. Do you comprehend how much you need to be grateful for? Understand and appreciate that, start from there, and then build a plan. Do you realise how relevant you are to Mom and us three kids? We love you, Pop. Just chill.' And, before the conversation could get more maudlin, Mimi's cell phone rang insistently. With another kiss to Pop's cheek, Mimi was off.

Left to his thoughts, Suresh had an epiphany. 'Aha, if anything, that's the message of this plague—be grateful. Maybe I should list all the things to be grateful about?'

Suresh grabbed a sheet of A4 paper and his Mont Blanc pen and started writing furiously. After a while, this is what was written on the sheet of paper:

I AM GRATEFUL FOR

1. *Having Sujata by my side holding my hand through thick and thin.*
2. *Me and the family all being healthy and untouched by the plague.*
3. *Sufficient funds providing me and the family with a good life.*
4. *Great circle of friends thankfully untouched by the plague.*
5. *A beautiful house that I love.*

6. *Children who are happy, successful, independent, and doing well in their careers.*
7. *The beautiful sunrise and sunset that I get to see every day.*
8. *The benevolence of nature surrounding me.*
9. *The fact that my elder sister who has suffered through a bad marriage and illness is now stable and is enjoying her life.*
10. *For just being alive and breathing.*

Suresh then carefully read what he had written and realised he was smiling. He turned to look at himself in the mirror and said aloud, addressing himself sternly, 'Be grateful.'

THE OTHER SIDE

Mayur was very excited. The broker had just handed over the keys of flat 62 at The Deluxe in Bandra West. This was his first property purchase, and he was extremely proud of himself. Straight out of IIM Calcutta, he had joined HSBC as a relationship manager and very quickly, in seven years, moved from branch manager to head of retail banking. At just 32 years of age, he was a self-funded property owner, and that was definitely to be regarded as an achievement. Yes, the EMI was pretty steep and, although the instalment payments for the apartment were to be stretched over 15 years, Mayur had a steady job with HSBC and a promising future in the banking industry. That would ensure that he would be able to honour his mortgage commitment to the bank.

As he drove to the apartment with Aramis, his cocker spaniel, sitting next to him, Mayur felt elated. Aramis, too, seemed very happy with the drive; the window was down and Aramis, with his face out of the window, had his tongue hanging out as the wind blew in his face, ruffling his hair.

As they entered the lobby of The Deluxe, both Mayur and Aramis paused to take in its subtle grandeur. It was truly a deluxe experience. A double-storied marble-tiled lobby with a huge wrought-iron chandelier, plush sofas, and plants in large brass pots. The Deluxe had a fully-equipped gymnasium and spa, an Olympic-size temperature-controlled swimming pool, and even a mini theatre that could seat 35 people. The entire west-facing rooftop, with its majestic view of the Arabian Sea and its spectacular sunsets, had been converted into an open-air lounge.

The concierge hurried up to Mayur with a welcoming smile, escorted him and Aramis to the elevator, and pressed the button for the sixth floor. There were two apartments on each landing. Mayur enquired about the owners of flat 61. The concierge mentioned that they were NRIs from Dubai, a Punjabi family that hardly ever visited India, and that the apartment remained closed most of the time.

As soon as they stepped out of the elevator onto the sixth-floor landing, Aramis started whimpering. With his tail between his legs, he tried running back into the elevator. When Mayur scooped him into his arms, he started barking wildly at the door of flat 61. Mayur was a little perturbed for a minute, but the excitement of stepping into his new house as the concierge threw open the door of flat 62 was too heady a moment to miss.

'At last, a home that I can call my own,' he thought, as he stepped into the flat as its newest owner.

The next month was a flurry of activity. Mayur assigned the cumbersome task of moving to Writers Relocators, who took over the project with gusto. Within a week, the new house was fully functional, with the kitchen and the bedroom furniture all in place. The living room had a sofa with two side tables and a large square coffee table in the centre, on Mayur's beloved Persian carpet. In one corner was the main piece of furniture—a well-stocked bar. Other than that, the living room was bare. Mayur would have to furnish it over time. He smiled with contentment to himself, quite satisfied with the move.

On the day of the intended first night at the flat—the formal move-in day—Mayur scheduled a pooja in the apartment and invited all his friends and family. This was Aramis' second trip to the flat and he reacted in the same strange manner as he had when he had visited a month back. As soon as the elevator door opened on the sixth floor and they stepped out, Aramis started whimpering and tried to get back into the elevator. Then, when Mayur picked him up, Aramis kept barking at the door of flat 61 until they entered flat 62, after which he seemed to settle down.

The pundit arrived an hour earlier than the guests. As he set up his pooja essentials, he complimented Mayur on the excellent vaastu of the house. The centrepiece of the pooja was a coconut placed upon a copper holder, and the pundit busied himself with setting up fruits and flowers around the copper holder.

The doorbell rang. Mayur's parents had arrived, carrying a huge bouquet of flowers, a Bohemian crystal vase that Mayur placed on the coffee table, and two boxes of Mayur's favourite vada. Mayur quickly hid one box of vadas in the fridge to be savoured by him exclusively at leisure in his solitude, as he gave his mother a quick conspiratorial smile and gave the second box to the pundit.

The guests started streaming in for the ceremony, and the house was filled with laughter, love, and bonhomie. As everyone gathered around the pundit, he started the pooja with the opening Sanskrit shlokas. At the end of every verse, Mayur and his parents had to dip their finger in vermillion paste and apply it to the head of the coconut. About 15 minutes into the ceremony, just as thepundit's chanting rose to a crescendo, signalling the end of the pooja, there was a loud crackle and, to everybody's consternation, the coconut cracked open. The pundit stopped his chanting for a brief second and then carried on as if nothing had happened, although his face revealed his true feelings.

The ceremony came to a close, and the guests got up to leave. Mayur had arranged a takeaway box containing a samosa, some mithai, and wafers, which was handed over to each guest as they were leaving. As the last guest left, Mayur's mother came up to him wearing a very concerned expression. The pundit wanted to talk to the three of them.

'Let me get straight to the point. There is some very wrong energy in this house,' the punditji said. 'To get rid of it, we will need to conduct a havan immediately. I have the requisite essentials to conduct the havan right away. Shall I start now?'

Mayur and his parents sat down for the havan, which was completed without any untoward incident. Mayur walked the pundit to the elevator.

'Enjoy your new home, Mayur. I sense a clearing of the negative energy in the house. But please be vigilant. Should you sense anything odd, please don't hesitate to call me,' was the pundits parting message as the elevator door closed.

Mayur's parents also left and, as his mother hugged him goodbye, being the ever-positive person she was, she said, 'Don't worry, son, all will be perfect.'

His father, being the atheist he was, said, 'Humbug! These things just happen. You cannot pay any attention to this nonsense, son.' But, as Mayur turned around to walk back into flat 62, he could not shrug off an overwhelming feeling of dread that seemed to have seeped into his being.

The evening passed quietly. Mayur slouched on the couch and watched the Indian cricket team battle it out with Australia at Lord's. India won the match in a nail-biting finish. Mayur headed to the kitchen, filled Aramis' bowl with the Royal Canin kibble that Aramis loved, and placed the bowl near the sofa so that the two of them could watch the box. Mayur then went back to the kitchen and rustled up a quick dinner for himself; noodles and meatballs was the order of the day. He then switched off the kitchen light and made himself comfortable on the couch to watch the news.

Suddenly, he heard Aramis barking loudly as he stood at the kitchen door, looking into the darkened kitchen. Aramis then started retreating while continuing to bark and stare at the kitchen as if he could see someone or something. His tail was between his legs; he looked really scared.

Mayur ran to pacify him, picked him up, stepped into the kitchen, and switched on the light. Fora brief instant just before the lights came on, Mayur sensed a presence and a flash of something undefined. For a moment, he too was afraid and stood stock-still. Then, telling himself he had just imagined it all and that Aramis' reaction was purely about getting accustomed to a new house, Mayur rationalised what had just occurred and headed back to the sofa to watch the news.

The rest of the evening was uneventful and, as Mayur settled down in his new bed for his first night in flat 62, he mulled over the events of the day. The pooja had gone well, but the pundits warning and Aramis' reaction had unsettled him more than he was willing to admit. 'Let's not overthink this one. It's just all about getting used to a new place and we both are just imagining things,' he muttered to himself as he turned to his right to assume his favourite curled-up position in bed. In less than a minute, Mayur was in the arms of Morpheus, fast asleep.

The next week was hectic. Mayur visited The Living Room to select and order the rest of his furniture. He had lunch on Thursday with his parents, and his mother helped him with the purchase of utensils, crockery, and cutlery; all of that was purchased on Amazon.

'Son, I am giving you a choice of the Wedgewood set or the Royal Doulton, so decide and let me know so that I can pack it up for you. Both the sets are anyway finally yours, so you may as well take one now and start using it for special occasions just as I do,' she said as she looked upon her son lovingly. Then, with a furtive look around to make sure Mayur's father was not listening, she quickly asked, 'Have there been any strange or untoward incidents at the apartment, son?'

Mayur decided not to divulge the events of the first night in Flat 62. It would unnecessarily upset his mother and, more importantly, he had not experienced any further odd happenings in the apartment since that night. 'No, Ma,' he said, 'all is good.' He hugged her and headed for the door.

The furniture delivery was scheduled for eleven a.m. on Monday. At about 10:55 a.m., Mayur headed to the service lobby of The Deluxe to supervise the unloading. As he exited the main lobby, a very pretty young woman about his age with a shih tzu on a leash passed him in the corridor. She hesitated for a minute, then smiled and extended her hand for a handshake.

'You must be Mayur Shah,' she said, 'the new owner of flat 62. I am Tanya Mistry of flat 52. I live directly below you. Welcome to The Deluxe.' As she shook his hand, it seemed she had a pressing question she wanted to ask him. Then, apparently deciding not to do so, Tanya just smiled and walked ahead.

Finally, all the new furniture was assembled and placed in the selected spaces and, at about six p.m., the delivery and assembly men left. As Mayur shut the door behind them, he surveyed the now fully-furnished living room. It looked good. Just then, his cell phone rang. It was Tanya.

'Hi Mayur, are you free for a drink this evening? This is very impromptu and I am so sorry for this last-minute invitation, but some of our building folks are collecting at my place at eight p.m. for drinks and finger food. We would really like you to join us.'

'Thanks for inviting me, Tanya,' Mayur responded. 'I will definitely be there. See you soon.'

At eight p.m., Mayur rang the doorbell of flat 52. A maid opened the door with a namaste and ushered him into a very tastefully furnished living room. Tanya rose up to greet him with a warm smile and introduced him to Preeti and Satish, a young married couple from flat 31 and Fareed, a 34-year-old investment banker from flat 72. After the initial back and forth about each other, the conversation was all about the building and the shameful carelessness of the Managing Committee. They all wanted more done about security.

'The security chap in the main lobby was fast asleep in his chair last night when we got back at three a.m., can you believe it?' Preeti raged.

'And what about cleaning and polishing?' Fareed complained. 'No one is supervising anything. Soon this fabulous building will become a slum like Dharavi.'

The evening was going well, with lots of laughter and friendly banter, and Mayur realised that he had found a community of like-minded people.

Suddenly Satish turned to Mayur and said, 'You are a brave person to buy flat 62, Mayur. You have real balls, man.'

All of a sudden, the room was enveloped in an uncomfortable silence.

Mayur gave Satish a blank stare.

'Are you trying to tell us you don't know about it, Mayur?' Satish gave Mayur a confused look.'Seriously?' Then, looking at the others, Satish added, 'He needs to know, guys, he can't be left in the dark.'

Tanya quickly added that they didn't know fact from fiction and in her opinion a lot was hearsay.

'In which case,' Satish said, 'let me break it up as such.'

Facts: there had been a death in flat 61 about six years back. The flat was occupied by the Mehra family. Father, mother, and a 24-year-old daughter, Prerna. The daughter's body was found outside the building in front of the main lobby. The police investigated the matter and closed the case, listing it as a suicidal death. The Mehras could not take the gossip and pain and moved to Dubai. The apartment was never sold.

Hearsay: Prerna was murdered. The apartment was haunted. No caretaker would agree to clean the apartment because they claimed they could hear whispers and objects seemed to move about without any propulsion. Mayur was the third owner of flat 62. The previous two owners had left because Prerna's spirit apparently visited flat 62 regularly. Moving objects, loud whispers in the night, the sound of someone sobbing, and at times even an apparition. In general, nobody wanted to be on or near the sixth-floor landing.

'That's it in summary,' Satish said. Then, looking at Mayur's face, which had turned white in shock, he added, 'Are you okay, bro?'

Tanya rushed to get Mayur a glass of water as Mayur struggled to compose himself.

'Guys, this has shaken me to the roots,' Mayur stuttered in shock, 'not only because I had no prior knowledge of this incident, but because I have experienced several strange events in my flat ever since I moved in.' Mayur proceeded to recount the entire incident with the punditji, Aramis' strange behaviour, and his own experience in the kitchen.

There was pin-drop silence when Mayur finished. The four of them looked at Mayur with great concern. Everyone had a different take on how to handle the matter; from *learn to deal with it*, to *do a havan in flat 62*, to *do a havan in flat 61*, and, very simply, *sell and leave*. The party quickly disbanded after that, and, as Tanya walked Mayur to the door, she gave him a goodnight peck on the cheek and said, 'Hang in there, mon ami, you will resolve this.'

Mayur returned to flat 62 and, as he closed the door, he realised he was deeply disturbed and had no clarity on how to deal with the situation. Aramis was glad to see him back and Mayur quickly changed into his nightclothes and settled himself in bed for the night. Very quickly, they both fell asleep.

Suddenly, Mayur sat up. He could hear Aramis whimpering, and he could see a depression in the bed next to where he slept, as if somebody was sitting next to him. Then he heard someone sobbing bitterly and a loud whisper that seemed to resonate around the room. 'Justice, justice, justice,' the voice said. Mayur leaned over and put on the bedside light. He realised his hands were shaking as he reached out to Aramis and hugged him. He quickly picked Aramis up and headed towards the door and exited the room. The door banged shut and, as he turned around, he saw the apparition clearly this time. It was a young girl, looking beseechingly at him.

'Justice, justice,' the apparition said to him.

Mayur screamed and covered his eyes. 'Go away, please go away,' he begged, and the apparition seemed to disappear and dissolve in front of him. Clutching Aramis, Mayur quickly left the bedroom, switched on all the lights in the house, and sat in the living room for the rest of the night, scared and trembling.

As dawn broke, Mayur felt his panic ebbing. He walked to the kitchen and fixed himself a mug of coffee. As he pondered the night's goings-on, he had a revelation: he realised that, although he was very scared, he somehow did not feel threatened by the apparition.

'She does not want to harm me,' he thought to himself. 'She just wants justice.'

Mayur was on cordial terms with Deepak Riberio, the Deputy Commissioner of Police. They had had extensive dealings with regard to a kidnapping case some years back. The kidnappers had asked for a ransom and Mayur had helped the DCP put it together. At eleven a.m. sharp Mayur called the DCP. He requested a meeting.

'Good to hear from you, Mayur. Does today three p.m. work for you? You know my office at Fort, let's meet there. Looking forward to catching up,' Deepak said.

Mayur walked into Deepak's office at three p.m. sharp. The DCP greeted him warmly and settled him down with a refreshing cup of masala tea. 'Tell me, my friend, how can I help you?' he said.

Mayur recounted the entire episode. 'I know this may sound absurd, but I am convinced that justice was not served in this case,' Mayur said.

Deepak looked at Mayur quizzically. 'I know you do not believe in ghosts and spirits normally, Mayur, it is not what I know of you; but given the fact that you feel it necessary to open the case; lets see what I can do. Please come back tomorrow at the same time and we will read the file together. Let me warn you, we need some substantive evidence or suspicion for us to advocate a reinvestigation of the case.' Deepak stood up to shake Mayur's hand and escorted him to the door.

Mayur drove back home deep in thought. His mother had introduced him to a clairvoyant, Aunty Sudha, at a party a year back. They had exchanged numbers. Maybe she could help.

'Aunty, this is Mayur, Kokilaben's son. Can I come and see you today? Sure, I can come right now.'

Sudha lived about two blocks from Mayur's place. As she ushered him into her sitting room and offered him a cup of green tea, she realised that Mayur was very agitated. Without much ado, Mayur swung into recounting the events and his opinion on the matter and that, although he was scared, he did not feel threatened by the apparition.

'There is an unresolved matter here, that is the sole reason for these manifestations,' he concluded.

Sudha quickly got up from her chair and headed towards the door. 'Take me to your apartment right now, Mayur,' she said. 'I need to talk to the spirit myself, as soon as possible, before this escalates out of control.'

As soon as they entered flat 62, Mayur perceived an eerie calm. He could see Aramis hiding under the sofa chair; he started whimpering as soon as he saw Mayur. The old familiar feeling of disquiet pervaded the room and Mayur sensed the spirit's presence.

'She is here,' he said as he turned to escort Sudha to the easy chair.

Sudha closed her eyes, seeming to collect herself and sharpen her focus. Then, after a minute, she opened her eyes and, looking towards a spot on the sofa opposite her, she said, 'Is that you, Prerna?'

There was an eerie silence for a minute, and then Prerna appeared, seated on the sofa. Aramis jumped into Mayur's lap as they both looked at the apparition of Prerna in fright. The sound of a tortured voice screaming 'Justice!' reverberated around the room.

Sudha addressed Prerna directly and came straight to the point. 'We need proof of a wrongdoing immediately to give to the police so that we can open up this case,' she told Prerna.

Prerna's spirit rose from the chair and went out through the main door of flat 62 onto the sixth-floor landing. Sudha and Mayur quickly opened the door and stepped onto the landing. Prerna was standing near the French windows in the lobby, pointing to a tile on the sill.

Mayur reluctantly stepped forward and, summoning all his courage and strength, tried to dislodge the tile, which abruptly came apart in his hand. In the niche created in the wall where the tile had been was an envelope. Mayur took the envelope, and both he and Sudha headed back to the apartment. As they turned around to enter flat 62, the apparition dissolved in front of their eyes.

Prerna's sad tale had been recorded in a typed-out letter addressed to the DCP, written anonymously. The Mehras had hired 26-year-old Pallat (not his real name) in early 2014. Prerna had found him the most strapping, well-built Pahadi that she had ever seen. Unbeknownst to her parents, as soon as they settled in for the night, Pallat would enter Prerna's room, at least three times a week, and the two of them would engage in wild, passionate sex. Yes, it was not lovemaking but a totally satisfying lustful escapade.

Prerna had developed a deep addiction to Pallat. On August 10, 2014, Prerna's parents had gone out for a family dinner. Prerna had complained of a headache and stayed back. As soon as her parents had left the house, Pallat had entered her room and the two of them had started a long, wild bout of sex. They had lost track of time, and, suddenly, Prerna had noticed her room door swing open and her father at the door, looking at the two of them in shock and disgust. Her dad had screamed in anger as Pallat had run out of the room and out of the main door, hastily pulling on his pants. Both her parents had entered the room, and she had covered herself and run into the bathroom to change. When she emerged, they had called her into the living room. Her father had started beating her with a belt while her mother tried holding him back. In the melee that ensued, they had reached the open window in the living room.

As she tried to stop her father from hitting her, he had pushed her back and she had tumbled over the sill to the ground below, at first hitting a ledge on the third floor that broke her fall. Miraculously, she did not die immediately. She had been clutching her cell phone and, in her last, fleeting moments, as she lay dying, she had called Pallat. The envelope contained the tale of her death in her own gasping testimony, as recorded by Pallat on his phone. Pallat did not want to be involved, but he wanted justice for Prerna or at least the world to know what had occurred. Pallat had hidden the envelope in the niche created by the tile, which in the past had been the post box for their secret communications, and he had sent an anonymous text message to the DCP that had obviously not reached the latter.

Both Sudha and Mayur looked sadly at each other. 'You must hand this over to the DCP tomorrow,' Sudha said. Mayur nodded wordlessly.

The next morning, Mayur walked into DCP Deepak Riberio's office. Deepak's secretary let him in to see Deepak immediately. 'You are lucky today, sir, he is free. No meetings,' the secretary said with a smile.

Deepak seemed immersed in a file and looked up in surprise. 'You are early today, Mayur.'

Mayur sat down and handed over the envelope. After Deepak had read the letter from Pallat and heard the tape, he looked up and said, 'This is a clear case of manslaughter. We will investigate this and get back to you. But how did you get this?' He tapped on the envelope.

Mayur recounted the entire experience with Aunty Sudha as Deepak looked at him incredulously.

'Okay, whatever the source,' Deepak said, 'we will pursue this.'

On his way home, Mayur felt elated. He had achieved something. The next couple of days, however, were uneventful. On the morning of the fourth day, Mayur got up and entered the bathroom to brush his teeth, and, as he straightened up after spitting into the sink, he saw the apparition of Prerna looking at him in the mirror. He froze.

'Just came back to thank you, Mayur,' Prerna whispered softly. 'I won't be bothering you anymore.' As Mayur turned around, the apparition dissolved in front of his eyes.

Mayur stepped out unsteadily and fixed himself a cup of coffee, then walked to the main door and picked up the newspaper lying outside. It was front page news. The police had tracked down Pallat—real name Arjun Pahadi—and recorded his testimony. The police had then contacted Mrs Mehra in Dubai and had recorded her testimony. Mr Mehra had expired of a heart attack a year ago and taken the secret of Prerna's death to his grave. The case was closed. But the truth of Prerna's death was out in the open, and her spirit could now rest in peace.

The calls started coming in, one after another. Aunty Sudha, Mayur's parents, the building friends Tanya, Preeti, Satish, Fareed—all congratulating him on a happy ending.

And when Mayur walked towards the windowsill of his sixth-floor flat and looked down at the ground below, he ruminated about his experience with the other side.

'All this has taught me that there is no need to fear death. What happens when we die can only be known when we do die. Till then, enjoy every minute of this gorgeous journey. There is so much that we don't know and don't understand,' he thought to himself.

'It was nice meeting you, Prerna, God bless,' Mayur said aloud as he turned away from the window.

MAKING IT WORK

Lying back on his recliner, Javed thought to himself, 'This is really a strange way to live. I had made a great retired life for myself. Using the club gymnasium thrice a week—treadmill, cycle, sauna, and the steam room—followed by a lazy breakfast in the Patio'—the restaurant in the club veranda overlooking the beautiful marina—'savouring the joy of watching the boats sailing by whilst tucking into the delicious fare of bun maska and egg bhurji with sips of masala tea. Divine. Then two hours in the club library catching up on the news, reading the newspapers and all the latest magazines. Absolutely perfect, I should say.'

Javed sighed deeply and stirred on the recliner. 'Let's go make some masala tea,' he said to Flopsy, his companion shih tzu. As Javed walked to the kitchen with Flopsy trotting alongside him, he recalled the dinners four times a week with friends at new restaurants, the theatre evenings at NCPA followed by dinner at the club, the Saturday family lunches at the Willingdon, and the Sunday lunch and a movie with his sister Latifa. It had been a wonderful life.

All this had been cruelly snatched away by the worldwide pandemic, during which the mantra had been to 'stay home' and 'stay safe'. Javed, unfortunately, was in the highest risk bracket, highly susceptible to infection by the virus. He was 64 years old, blood group A+, with chronic diabetes, blood pressure, and hypertension. He had been advised not to venture out until both a treatment and a preventive to overcome the virus was available, and he had been homebound for over 90 days, except for the occasional trip to the bank and to take Flopsy to Dr Deepak at VetClinic.

'How is a 90 days plus lockdown;; wherein one is restricted to the boundaries of one's apartment, supposed to work for anybody?' Javed voiced aloud to Flopsy, who gave him his standard quizzical stare. Granted, Javed by his very intrinsic nature was not a very sociable person and enjoyed his 'personal space', as he chose to call the time he spent by himself. His regular mantra had always been that he quite enjoyed his own company. He was a voracious reader and a jazz afficionado; both hobbies kept him more than occupied. 'And if I have to sacrifice my "me time", the people I am with better be worth the time and effort,' he would often say to his friends. He abhorred large parties where everybody talked at the same time and there was no real sharing of experiences or ideas; merely a façade of posturing and positioning. So he could not understand why the limitations of the lockdown did not work for him.

'No man is an island,' Javed advised Flopsy. 'That quotation is so true.' Javed then searched the net for the full quotation. It was a quotation from John Donne's *Devotions* (1624): 'No man is an island, entire of itself, every man is a piece of the Continent, a part of the main.'

Yes, Javed did enjoy being by himself, but he did need human interaction, places to visit, and events to attend to add flavour to his life. Yes, the weekly video chats on the phone with the various groups did help, but that was not a substitute for actual physical interaction. All said and done, he did want to be and was a 'piece of the continent'.

It was Thursday. Javed ruminated on the long day ahead of him. He was truly tired of watching Netflix, reading, and listening to music. 'To enjoy leisure time, one must be busy doing something that requires an application of cognitive thinking. These endless ennui-filled days are getting to be stifling,' he thought to himself. 'So what can one do to make life more interesting?' He decided to check out *A Long Walk to Freedom*—Nelson Mandela's autobiography. Nelson Mandela was locked in a cell for over 20 years; perhaps his book would give Javed an insight into how best one could deal with restrictions on movement.

The book highlighted that prison life was all about routine. During the day, they were out in the open, breaking stones in a lime quarry. Evenings were about walks in the courtyard, after which there was an hour of reading, with lights out at nine thirty p.m. But that was exactly the issue. The need to define and set up a daily routine within the confines of the apartment was proving to be a difficult task. As mentioned in the book, it required the mind to be strong and to control the emotional upheavals that he was experiencing. From complete laziness to boredom, resulting in a desire to stay inert. Doing nothing.

'So let's see,' Javed mulled. 'What kind of routine can I set for myself? Something that will make me feel fulfilled?' He grabbed a writing pad and a pen and decided to write down a typical daily routine that he could follow:

8.30 am	*Rise and shine*
8.30 to 9.30 am	*Shit, shave and shampoo*
9.30 am to 10 am	*Call Latifa*
10 am to 10.30 am	*Breakfast*
10.30 am to 11.30 am	*Check out the news on the Internet*
11.30 am to 1.30 pm	*Writing and painting time*
1.30 pm to 2.00 pm	*Lunch*
2.00pm to 4.00 pm	*Siesta time*
4.00 pm to 5.00 pm	*Yoga and meditation*
5.00 pm to 7.00 pm	*TV time—Netflix and the like*
7.00 pm to 8.00 pm	*Video chat time*
8.00 pm to 9.00 pm	*Family time over a drink or two in the main hall*
9.00 pm to 9.30 pm	*Dinner*
9.30 pm to 11.30 pm	*Reading time*
11.30 pm	*Bedtime ... good night*

'That looks very workable, doesn't it, Flopsy?' said Javed. Flopsy yawned in agreement and continued to look at Javed in bewilderment.

The main issue was exercising the discipline required to follow this regimen. Javed would get up every morning with the intention of following a fixed pattern of behaviour, but, unfortunately, by the time he finished his breakfast he felt like doing nothing. Emotion overcame the desire to establish a structured pattern of living, and the day progressed with 'going with the flow.' There were also the normal household and banking matters to attend to. A simple exercise—letting a repairman into the house—became a huge, complicated task. The minute the technician left the house, the entire area where they had operated in had to be sanitised. Although this was carried out by the live-in staff, the protocol had to be supervised by Javed.

'When will we be done with this pandemic and revert back to normal?' Javed thought to himself. The way the scientific world was dealing with the vaccine was unnerving. It appeared no institution or scientific body had a clear idea of what the virus was about. Like a friend of Javed's had said in video chat, 'Man, can you believe it, despite all the money pumped in and the best minds in the world working on it for five months, nobody has been able to come out with a cure for a virus that dies on contact with soap.' Everybody was clueless, including the WHO, *especially* the WHO, with their constantly changing protocols. From *masks were useful* to *don't wear masks, they don't make a difference. The virus is not airborne* to *maybe the virus IS airborne. Don't wear gloves when going out* to *wear gloves when going out, they act as the first line of defence.* Clueless.

So this homebound existence would probably be the way ahead for the next one year. 'Who would have ever imagined at the beginning of 2020 that our lives would be contained and reduced to this?' Javed said aloud to himself.

Javed's cell phone buzzed impatiently. 'Hi, sir.' It was Pratap, Javed's wealth manager. 'We have a new hedge fund. It is a derivative-based scheme that I thought would interest you.' And, as Pratap launched into detailing the scheme, Javed thought to himself, 'In normal times, Pratap would be in my house talking to me and not promoting this scheme on a video chat. We created technology and globalised the planet to make things work better for us but this extreme connectivity has led to the swift transmission of everything, including a virus. How else could an outbreak in Wuhan, China, become a pandemic that has crippled the whole planet in five months and led to over half a million deaths worldwide? This technology has been a boon and a curse.'

Javed let Pratap finish his brief and then promised to get back to him if he was interested. It was only eleven a.m., and Javed had planned nothing for the day. The phone rang again. it was his cousin Ramila.

'Hi there, just called to check on your current electricity bill. My normal monthly bill is about Rs. 5,000. This bill is for Rs. 40,000. What do you think I should do?' Ramila sounded very perturbed.

Javed told Ramila to pay the bill and file a complaint with the relevant authority. The virus had led to a nationwide lockdown, and this had also affected the functioning of all support institutions. The reading of the electricity meters that recorded the consumption of electricity was manually performed by the electric company. Due to the virus, there were no electric technicians available to carry out the readings on the meter, and, even if they were available, most buildings were in self-imposed quarantine and were not permitting anybody onto their premises. This rule had only been relaxed that month; the readings had been taken only a week back, leading to these extreme bills. So now they would have to deal with increased costs on top of all this mayhem.

Javeds thought about his video chat last night with his friends based in London and Dubai. Their lives, although not so severely restricted in terms of movement by the government, were restricted by their own need for abundant precaution. They were both working from home, which kept them quite busy. In the last four months, they had visited friends only twice for dinner and had on those occasions sat out in the garden with social distancing. Although the UK and the UAE had opened up malls, cinemas, bars, hotels, and restaurants, neither of them had been to one since March 2020. 'Do not be scared, but be very aware and careful' was the overriding motto. It was their opinion that the lockdown would continue until at least December 2021; until a workable vaccine could be released to the public. That projection, they all agreed, was a very disturbing thought.

Javed switched on the television. NDTV was having a panel discussion on 'The New Normal'. Javed settled into his easy chair to watch. What was the new normal that would have to be lived with for the next 18 months? After passionate and vociferous arguments back and forth between the panellists, the conclusion was as follows:

For the next 18 months, until the vaccine is developed,

1. *Avoid crowds.*
2. *Go outside only if necessary.*
3. *Wear masks whenever you step out and sanitise your hands regularly.*
4. *When you return from stepping out, have a bath and sanitise your clothes.*
5. *Do not have more than two visitors over and make sure you are sitting in an open area or, if inside the house, with the windows open.*
6. *Work from home and hold webinars if need be, instead of going out.*
7. *Exercise regularly at home and video chat with your friends once a day.*

8. *Develop a hobby or interest; something new to teach yourself daily. Keep your mind and body active.*

9. *Eat healthy—lots of fruit and vegetables.*

'Where is the fun in all this?' Javed muttered to himself. The thought that human interaction had been reduced to video chat was pathetic. 'But you know what, so be it. When the going is tough, the tough get going. One can either be swamped by challenges or take it in one's stride and make life interesting.'

Javed walked to the mirror in the hall and spoke to his reflection: 'I will follow my routine and make it work. Life is a party and the best part is that it is always a roller coaster. So enjoy the journey.' Flopsy, watching this interaction, barked and wagged his tail in agreement.

NEIGHBOURS

The broker Kishore escorted Mehul and Aditi into Abana Apartments on Carmicheal Road. The façade of the three-storied building was very pretty, with trellised balconies, flower boxes overflowing in paroxysms of multi-hued flowers, a marbled lobby, stilt parking for two cars per flat, and high-speed elevators. Classic but contemporary was the overall style.

Mehul and Aditi were immediately attracted to the building. There were six apartments in it. Apartment number 5 on the third floor was up for sale. The current owner, Mr Mehra, was moving to Canada to live with his son and family. His son did not want to ever come back to India, so Mr Mehra was disinvesting and moving out.

Kishore rang the doorbell, and the three of them were ushered into the living room. The apartment had high ceilings and very tasteful period furniture. Mr Mehra invited them to inspect the house. He also confirmed that there were no termite problems, leakages, or water supply issues in the flat.

For Mehul and Aditi, it was love at first sight. They looked at each other and both knew that their search for an apartment had reached a happy conclusion. Masking their excitement and pretending to be nonchalant, they told Mr Mehra that Kishore would be in touch with him.

As soon as they sat in the car, they told Kishore to finalise the deal inclusive of all the period furniture. Kishore confirmed he would get back to them with a sale price very soon. Within a week, the transaction was completed and Mehul and Aditi had the keys to the flat.

Kishore then highlighted the protocol that needed to be followed with the other owners. Abana Apartments was a cooperative society under the Building Cooperative Societies Act. The owners were bound by the bylaws of the society and, to that effect, Mehul and Aditi as joint owners would have to sign many forms formalising their adherence to the bylaws—documents on stamp paper. Other than that, there would be a meeting with the chairman, secretary, and one other Managing Committee member, which was a mere formality. Mr Mehra had already cleared the sale to Mehul and Aditi with the Managing Committee or MC, as it was better known.

The MC meeting, although very formal, went very smoothly, and Mehul and Aditi were welcomed into the Abana community.

The first month was hectic. Settling into new premises is never an easy task. Mehul had toattend a conference in Paris for a week, so much of the burden of moving had to be shouldered by Aditi, who did a remarkably efficient job. Mehul returned from his conference and, as he stepped across the threshold of his new apartment, a deep sense of belonging and completeness overcame him. He walked to Aditi, who was in the kitchen, and hugged her tight.

'What is the matter, my love?' Aditi said as she hugged him back, understanding and reciprocating his deep emotion.

The next month was a flurry of housewarming parties. Their friends and family members loved the building and the apartment and showered them with compliments on finding a 'diamond', so to speak. The couple then decided to throw a housewarming for the other residents of the building. Aditi did not want to send Whatsapp invites or slip cards under their doors. She wanted to invite them personally. This, to Aditi's bewilderment, did not turn out to be the set of warm interactions that she had envisaged.

Monday morning was bright and pleasant. Mehul left for work at nine a.m., as per his normal schedule. Aditi got ready to visit all the building members to invite them for the housewarming party.

At eleven a.m., Aditi rang the doorbell to flat 1. There was no response for a while. Then, a female voice rang out through the speaker. Aditi realised that the apartment was connected to a surveillance camera, and she was required to respond.

'Hi, this is Aditi from flat 5. May I know who I am talking with?'

'This is Mrs. Faizulabhoy,' the disembodied voice said. 'What do you want?'

That was definitely rude and quite unfriendly.

'I wanted to invite you for dinner to my place on Sunday. We thought it would be a good idea to get to know the other residents of Abana.'

'We do not interact with Abana people so we will not be able to make it,' said the voice, after which the connection was abruptly cut.

Aditi was quite taken aback but she just shrugged her shoulders and muttered 'que sera sera' to herself. She then rang the bell to flat 2. The apartment had two doors—a tastefully designed black and gold metal-grilled door covered a mahogany wooden door.

'The residents of Abana are quite particular about their security. Maybe we, too, need to apply our minds to something similar,' Aditi thought to herself.

The wooden door swung open and a young maid faced Aditi. 'Yes, madam?'

Aditi explained that she was from flat 5 and asked if she could talk to the maid's madam.

The maid asked her to wait for just a minute and shut the door.

Very soon, the wooden door opened again and a very elegant older women with coiffured hair appeared.

'Hi, I am Meera, please do come in,' she said as she opened the metal door and welcomed Aditi into a living room with art décor furniture and some very beautiful Persian carpets. 'You are Aditi, are you not? Can I offer you a nice cup of masala tea?'

'What a welcome change from the earlier interaction,' Aditi thought to herself. 'I wanted to invite you for dinner at my place on Sunday at eight p.m.,' she said aloud with a sweet smile. 'I hope you can make it. Mehul felt it was time to get to know the Abana community better.'

'Of course, my dear, what a wonderful idea. We will definitely be there,' Meera said with much enthusiasm as she poured a cup of masala tea for Aditi.

Aditi then recounted the strange interaction that she had had with the tenant of flat 1.

With a solemn face, Meera responded, 'Poor dears. They are to be pitied. The family was originally husband Suresh and wife Mridula and a 19-year-old son Ajay. A tall, strapping, good-looking, and extremely popular lad who excelled both at academics and sports. The house was always filled with youngsters and merriment. Both Suresh and Mridula were very social, and my husband Dilip and I attended many entertaining dinners at their flat. About a year back, Ajay was returning home from a late-night party. He was driving too fast and could not control the car around a particularly sharp bend on the road. The car hit the side railing, overturned, and burst into flames. Ajay was killed instantly. With that, the light seemed to just disappear from flat 1. Suresh and Mridula stopped meeting people, stopped going out, and spent their time grieving deeply, just not being able to move on in life. The Abana community tried to help and reach out many times to offer solace but had the door slammed in our faces at each attempt. Finally, everybody decided to just let the couple be by themselves, hoping that one day they would be able to step out from the darkness.'

'That is terrible. Any words of comfort are inadequate. I feel so sad for them.' Aditi's eyes filled with tears. 'There is nothing really that one can say to the couple.'

After a brief chat about other, lighter topics, during which Aditi recounted the trials and tribulations of changing residences, she got up to leave, and, as Meera escorted her out, she confirmed, once again, that she and her husband Dilip would be at the dinner on Sunday.

Meera rang the doorbell of flat 3, the residence of Mr Agarwal, the chairman of the Abana Society. The door was opened by a petite, very traditionally-dressed elderly woman; she wore a sari, had a big red bindi on her forehead, sindoor in the middle parting of her hair, and a mangalsutra around her neck. She seemed to recognise Aditi immediately.

'Agarwalji is not at home,' she said with a smile. 'Maybe I can help you?' But she did not invite Aditi into the apartment. Aditi could smell the fantastic aromas of Indian cooking wafting out of the kitchen. She invited Mrs Agarwal, who, as was expected, said she would convey the message to 'Agarwalji', who would get back to Aditi. She then closed the door with a smile.

Aditi walked across the landing and rang the doorbell to flat 4, which housed the secretary of the Abana Society, Mrs. Vandana Gill. She was a middle-aged modern woman, a very successful interior designer who ran her business from her apartment. The door opened almost immediately, Vandana was on the phone and gestured to Aditi that she would take just a minute.

'Hi Aditi, sorry, today being Monday is a crazy busy day, how can I help?' Vandana said as her phone rang stridently once again. Aditi quickly extended the invite, and Vandana confirmed they would be there as she apologetically turned away to take the call and shut the door.

Aditi then walked up to the third floor and rang the bell to apartment 6, her neighbour across the landing. In the past month, she had met Shirley and Babar on the landing and had exchanged pleasantries about settling in and the weather. Shirley and Babar had invited Mehul and Aditi for dinner on one occasion, but they could not accept the invitation because they had commitments elsewhere on the same date. Shirley and Babar had two grown-up kids who had settled in the US, and the couple visited their children and family for three months every year. The apartment was locked up for three months, but every week a trusted cleaning lady would collect the keys from the Agarwals to clean the house. Shirley was a homemaker and Babar was a very hardworking exporter of dry fruits with a retail outlet on Napean Sea Road.

Shirley opened the door and invited Aditi into her apartment. It was a very dark coloured apartment, old style furniture, old paintings on the wall, maroon curtains and maroon velvet upholstery. 'I would be so depressed living in a house like this,' Aditi thought to herself.

Shirley very graciously confirmed that she and Babar would be there on Sunday. It was nearly lunch time by then, and Aditi had a hair appointment at the salon—Mehul's boss had invited them over for dinner—so she quickly excused herself and left. Shirley chatted with her until the elevator came up then waved and shut her door.

Saturday and Sunday morning went by in a flurry of activity as Aditi had to cook for 10 people. They had a 12-seater dining table that had to be set up with the right crockery and cutlery. Mehul was in charge of the bar and had ordered the whole range of spirits, from wines to Scotch. And before they knew it, Sunday eight p.m. was almost upon them. They quickly got ready to welcome their guests. Mehul and Aditi were well aware of the importance of first impressions and wanted their neighbours to think well of them.

The first guests to ring the bell of flat 5 were Agarwalji and his wife. Aditi welcomed them warmly, got them seated, and served them fresh coconut water, which was what they had requested. Mehul and Agarwalji were soon debating the new Finance Act and seemed to hit it off very well.

By nine p.m., all the guests had arrived and were satisfactorily ensconced in the living room and deep in conversation with each other. After a couple of drinks, as was always the case, the conversation grew more animated, the laughter got louder, and a great sense of bonhomie pervaded the room. Each apartment had its own story to recount. They all had children and, in every case, the children lived outside India. The parents visited their kids once a year or once in two years.

Mehul asked Meera why she did not move to the United States of America instead of living in Abana. Before Dilip could respond, Meera gave a very befitting reply, throwing her head back and laughing as she said, 'Why on earth would we want that? My son and his wife would be out at work. The kids would be at school and Satish and myself would have to talk to the dog and the parrot. We are far better off living in Abana. We have friends to meet up with, there are cousins who visit quite often, and we have the Willingdon Club to keep us entertained. Living in the US with our son and family would not be an option even if I outlived Satish and was by myself.'

Meera's words seemed to resonate with the rest of the guests, who apparently were in the same situation. Mehul continued topping up the glasses of the six guests with wine and Scotch, with the exception, obviously, of the Agarwals, who were on their third glasses each of coconut water. The guests were having a great time.

Aditi announced dinner at ten thirty p.m. The cuisine was a mixture of Chinese and Indian food. Aditi and their live-in cook Malti had prepared all the dishes, and, very soon, there were loud exclamations of how tasty the food was. The guests congratulated Aditi with great gusto.

After dinner, Mehul suggested cognac or liqueurs. Two of the guests opted for cognac and three guests opted for Drambuie. Soon after, it was midnight, at which time all eight guests got up to go, thanking Mehul and Aditi for a wonderful party and complimenting them for being such exceptional hosts.

Meera said to all, 'This was so much fun. We must have the next one at my place. I will be in touch.'

After the last guest had left and Mehul had locked the doors, both of them sprawled out on the sofas, looked at each other and smiled in satisfaction.

'That went off really well, baby, the food was excellent,' Mehul said. 'Our real introduction to the Abana community was achieved today. I think they liked us.'

You can change friends but not neighbours.

ATAL BIHARI VAJPAYEE

RETIREMENT

It was a great feeling of freedom tinged with immense relief. Today was Adil's 60th birthday and he had decided to resign. As Adil handed over his resignation with some trepidation to the CEO he quietly waited for a response.

Mithun, the CEO, looked up and smiled. 'I have been expecting this for quite a while, my dear chap. Are you sure this is what you want?'

Adil nodded his head silently. It had been 35 years of hard, back-breaking work. The targets to be achieved, sometimes seemingly impossible, the minefield of corporate politics to be managed, and the constantly high stress levels had affected Adil's health. All put together, it had reached a zenith of complete suffocation. Adil had had enough. It definitely was time to explore an alternative lifestyle. A more sedentary, peaceful existence.

Mithun looked at Adil kindly. 'I accept your resignation, Adil. You will be missed. Blessings always and please do drop in for a chat from time to time.' The two of them got up and shook hands, and Adil thanked Mithun as he headed for the door.

One month later, Adil opened his eyes from a deep and fitful sleep. It was six thirty a.m., his normal wake-up time. This was the first day of his retirement. He literally had the whole day stretching ahead of him with nothing planned. After a life of 14-hour workdays, it felt blissful. He then decided to plan his day. He would call Rohit, his schoolmate, and discuss matters with him further. Rohit had suggested that Adil could join his work team as an office administrator. It was unsaid but apparent that this would be a voluntary appointment. A win-win situation for all.

Adil arrived at Rohit's office at about noon. Rohit's aide Shalini took Adil around the office. It was a renowned event management company called LEAVE IT TO US. Rohit was the sole proprietor. LEAVE IT TO US managed theme parties, musical gigs, and weddings, both local and destination. The office was a compact unit in Express Towers, Nariman Point, and housed a small team of 35 highly skilled and experienced staff members. Since much of the staff spent their workdays outside the office, there were 35 workstations with four large rooms in each of the corners of the office.

Shalini ushered Adil into a corner room overlooking the sea and said, 'This will be your office, sir. And now Rohit Sir would like you to join him for lunch. Can you please follow me?' She led the way into Rohit's tastefully decorated office.

Rohit was on the telephone, but he immediately cut his conversation and reached out to hug Adil warmly. 'Malti has made a special lunch with all the dishes that you like,' he said, as he led Adil to a walnut wood table in one corner of his office. The office boy walked in to set the table. Adil was a favourite of Rohit's wife; Malti found him incredibly polished, erudite, and knowledgeable.

Lunch was delicious, and the two friends started discussing the areas in which Rohit wanted Adil to apply his skills. Documentation, logistics, and coordination were critical areas of weakness within LEAVE IT TO US. Each project was managed by a representative who behaved pretty much like a law unto themselves, citing deadlines as the overriding criterion for their messy and incomplete documentation.

Rohit never seemed to know what liabilities the representatives had undertaken for the LEAVE IT TO US projects. He did trust them implicitly, but he now wanted protocols defined that would capture the liabilities on paper as soon as they were undertaken. Logistics and coordination were other essentials, so for each project Rohit wanted a budget and a time and activity chart to be submitted to Adil prior to its commencement so that Adil could monitor the progress of the project on a weekly basis.

At the moment, all this was done informally in conversations during the weekly team meetings that Rohit conducted. The challenging task ahead and the main hurdle to overcome would be the mindset of the representatives. Adil would need to cajole them into accepting and applying the new protocols.

The next morning, Adil was at his desk by eleven a.m., working diligently on his computer. Within the week, he had written up the protocols with attached formats and had got Rohit to approve of the same with some minor changes. Rohit then called a meeting of all the staff members for the following Monday.

Monday dawned as a blisteringly hot day. When Rohit got to the office, he could see all the 35 representatives at their desks. The buzz of conversation died down as soon as Rohit and Adil walked into the room.

Rohit opened the meeting by first highlighting the excellent job the team was doing. He also emphasised his deep trust in their integrity and professionalism, but pointed out that, as the owner of the business, he could not be in a situation wherein he did not know where and to what extent each project was going. Rohit then introduced Adil, and Adil started defining the new protocols. Each representative was given a USB stick with the protocols. Rohit then ended the meeting, adding that this was an attempt not to micromanage the project or put shackles on the creative juices of the staff but merely to be able get an understanding of the project while it was being conducted and not only when it was completed.

The team was quiet when Rohit finished. Adil then asked Shalini to set up one-on-one meetings with each of the 35 representatives. The meetings took the better part of the whole week and went off very well. The representatives seemed to understand the need for the new protocols and some even felt it would make their work run more smoothly.

Before he knew it, six months had flown past. The protocols had been implemented and the process was running smoothly to the benefit and satisfaction of all. Adil realised that he was now bored with the monotony of the work. He had trained Shalini in monitoring and mapping processes, and she was doing the task very efficiently. Adil realised he was looking for a new challenge. He expressed his restlessness to Rohit, who said, 'I knew this was coming. Please feel free to explore any other avenues you desire to. And thank you so very much for the work you have done here. I will always be grateful to you, mon ami.'

That night, Adil and his college batchmates met at the Willingdon Club for dinner. The conversation centred around giving back to the community. That piqued Adil's curiosity immediately. Ramesh, his batchmate, suggested that Adil should involve himself with the NGO that Ramesh had started. Its focus was education for rural children and the first group meeting was scheduled for eleven a.m. the following Saturday.

Adil met the NGO team of seven members, who hailed from a varied diaspora and had a wide range of accumulated experience, at their office on Saturday. The main item on the agenda had to do with defining the profiles and skill sets of the online teachers. The children assembled in a set of four rooms, each of which accommodated 25 children of similar ages. The rooms in the village had been rented by the NGO and each room had a middle-aged class monitor who had been recruited from the village on a salary paid for by the NGO. The classes were conducted online, Monday to Friday.

The discussion was animated and exciting and Adil went home quite fulfilled. He felt he was contributing towards something worthwhile and far bigger than himself. For the initial months, Adil attended all the Saturday meetings of the NGO. He even visited the village classes to understand the impact the NGO was having on the schoolchildren. However, at the end of six months, Adil felt the dissatisfaction with his life seeping in once again.

Other than Saturdays, which were devoted to the NGO, Adil filled his weekdays with reading, music, attending the theatre, and meeting friends at the club or at restaurants. But what Adil realised was that he was merely finding ways to fill his days and nothing so far had encompassed his attention. He was constantly restless. He could not imagine living another 20 years just trying to find ways to fill his days with activity. At such times, he felt it was time to transition; his journey of life had reached its end.

Little did he know that events would quickly overcome him and force hime to reassess his retired existence.

It started out as a mild but persistent stomach ache. Adil's GP suspected that it was an ulcer and recommended a 2D Doppler. To everybody's consternation, it was discovered that Adil had a tumour and was diagnosed as having first-degree pancreatic cancer. The radiation and chemotherapy started almost immediately and, because they had caught the cancer in its early stages, it quickly went into remission, and Adil was declared 'fit as a fiddle.' The treatment had stretched for over two months, and Adil had had a lot of time to ruminate on dealing with his retirement, to search for answers regarding the way forward. Then, one cloudless, blue morning, whilst sipping his first cup of tea and looking at the blue sea in front of him from his balcony, Adil was hit by a sudden epiphany. Everything was suddenly crystal clear.

Retirement was like a gift. If you were fortunate enough to stay healthy, you could use all this time at your disposal to fill your life with new experiences and memories, beyond the mundane targets of earning a living and tending to your family. So one must not complain about the 'sunset' years but relish them to the fullest.

With this new insight, Adil's days were now filled with new adventures. He had come to terms with his retired existence and, for the first time in many years, he was not restless anymore.

As with everything with us humans, and which is the irony of our lives, Adil had to fall seriously ill for him to understand and appreciate the gift of retirement. He needed a jolt to bring himself out of his self-indulgent stupor.

'Better late than never,' Adil thought to himself as he settled comfortably into his armchair and immersed himself in the latest bestseller.

COVERING ALL THE ODDS

As Greg drove Sid back to the hotel, Sid realised that he was truly exhausted. Waves of fatigue hit him hard.

Sid had arrived in Houston two days ago and, without giving himself any time to recover from his jet lag, he had swung into 48 hours of tough negotiations with Greg. Greg had finally acquiesced to the terms that Sid had proposed, and Sid couldn't wait to get into his room and just sleep—or 'hit the sack' as is often said.

As he turned the key to enter his hotel room, he heard the phone ringing stridently. Sid strode urgently to the bedside phone and picked up the receiver.

'Hi honey.' It was Sid's wife Ruby, calling from Mumbai. 'Are you seated, my love? I am afraid I have bad news. It's your mom—she left us five minutes back. You need to come back to India.'

As a deluge of emotions hit Sid, his mind started dealing with the logistics of heading back. Sid immediately called Greg, who asked Sid to pack his bag.

'My deepest condolences, Sid,' Greg said. 'I will meet you in the lobby and I will talk to the travel agent to put you on the quickest flight to Mumbai.'

The quickest flight that could be arranged was Houston–New York–Dubai–Mumbai, which departed from Houston in two hours. Greg drove Sid immediately to the airport, and Sid was literally the last person to check in to the Emirates flight out of Houston.

On the long journey to Mumbai, Sid's thoughts turned to his loving parents. Although he had not lived with his folks since he had moved out at 16 to go to college, he had always had a strong and binding connection with them. He had known that, come what may, they would always have his back. He would miss his mom deeply, her unconditional love and the way her eyes lit up every time she saw him.

'How will Dad manage without Mom?' Sid thought to himself. His parents had been married for 59 years and had been together for 66 years.

Ruby was at the airport to receive Sid, and, as she hugged him tight, Sid could not control his tears. The next few days were a whirl of religious ceremonies and as Sid released his mother's ashes into the Arabian Sea and bid farewell to his first love his thoughts turned to his father.

Sid's father Ram was 86 years old. A kind, erudite, fiercely independent, scholarly man, an atheist who had constantly lectured his children on the treachery of religion. 'Religion is for a weak and uncultivated mind,' he always said. 'It has been created by man and unleashes mankind's subdued venom on the planet. If a man tells you that he is truly religious, avoid him like the plague.' His dislike for religion and religious people was probably driven by the horrors of the Partition in 1947 that had torn the Indian subcontinent asunder and had uprooted him from his natural environment and forced him to make a new home in another city. 'Everything is here and now, there is no after. From dust to dust will you go. So remember, children, all you need to lead a rich, fulfilling life are good thoughts, good deeds, good actions. That should be your guiding mantra.'

The morning after the last religious ceremony, Sid fixed himself his morning coffee and stepped out on to the terrace, where Ram was sipping his tea. Sid hugged his father, kissed him on his forehead, and sat opposite him, watching him in silence. Ram looked lost and seemed to have withdrawn within himself.

'Dad, may I suggest something? Why don't you come and live with Ruby and me in Dubai? I have told my office to arrange a resident visa for you.'

There was no response from Ram. Sid gave Ram a minute, then repeated his statement and added, 'Dad, please say something.'

Ram looked lovingly at his son. 'My dear, dear boy, I don't know how much time I have left, and I would like to spend my remaining years in this house with all its memories of the wonderful life I had with your mother.' Ram paused. 'I love you, my son.'

Sid's eyes welled with tears but he carried on doggedly. 'Then should Ruby and I move back to India and live with you in this house?'

Ram looked a little taken aback. 'Not at all, Sid, you have your own life to lead and I mine. But I truly appreciate your caring.' He got up and gave Sid a tight hug.

Ruby, who had stepped on to the terrace and had overheard the conversation, added, 'Dad, please come and stay with us in Dubai.'

Ram wordlessly stepped back into the living room and, while passing Ruby, placed his hand on her head in a silent blessing. He then headed back to his room.

As Ruby tearfully stepped into Sid's arms for a hug, Sid thought aloud, 'Dad is too independent, my love. He will never agree to a change.'

Ram's home was a beautifully decorated art deco three-bedroom apartment that was attended to by Ramparsad the cook and Akbar the houseboy. Both Ramparsad and Akbar had worked with the family for over 10 years and were devoted to Ram. As Sid sat on the terrace deep in thought, watching Ramparsad and Akbar go about their morning chores, the two of them walked up to him.

Ramparsad, being the elder, took the lead, and, folding his hands in a namaste, he said, 'Saab, we beg you, don't be worried. We will take good care of Barra sahib. But can we suggest something. It would perhaps be a good idea if you came and checked on Barra sahib once every month.'

'Let me think about it,' Sid responded gratefully, getting up and clasping Ramparsad's hands. Akbar bent down to touch Sid's feet in the old Indian traditional manner of respecting a benefactor, and Sid blessed him by placing his palm on Akbar's forehead.

'This sounds workable,' Sid thought to himself. 'Need to plan the logistics.'

After a long discussion with Ruby, the plan was put into effect.

When Sid and Ruby retuned to Dubai and their jobs and lifestyles, Sid took to calling his father three times a day: after breakfast, lunch, and dinner. Short conversations filled with caring and family gossip, Ram's cynical point of view on world affairs and in general—attempts, as it were, to touch base. Additionally, on the last weekend of every month, Sid took the red eye out of Dubai on Thursday night enroute to Mumbai and out of Mumbai on Saturday night enroute to Dubai. Weekends in the Middle East were observed on Fridays and Saturdays.

On these monthly trips, Sid decided to sleep in the same bed as Ram, with Akbar sleeping on the floor next to them, as Akbar did every night to help Ram with his nightly visits to the bathroom. Father and son had long, soul-fulfilling chat sessions on these trips, fondly reminiscing about happy times spent together, especially with Sid's mother. Every morning, Sid would open his eyes and see Ram sitting on the sofa opposite the bed, sipping his tea and reading the paper. An hour of side-splitting laughter would follow that would have Sid literally tumbling out of the bed, as Ram in his inimitable style would reflect on the follies of the world and world leaders.

And on Saturday night, as Sid would step out to head back to Dubai, he would see his wizened old father sitting on the sofa chair, Akbar on a stool next to him, both watching television. He would think sadly to himself, 'I wish we could live together, but Dad wants his independence.'

Ram did not ever comment on anything that Sid did for him, but Sid's care did not go unnoticed. Ram's eyes said it all when he often looked gratefully and lovingly at his exemplary son and took to blessing Sid innumerable times by placing his palm over Sid's head.

There were a few memorable incidents that needed to be recounted.

It was a Monday morning in Dubai. Sid had called Mumbai to talk to his father. Sid would normally call after Ram's breakfast, but today he had an important meeting with the credit head of Citibank Dubai and the chairman of the group, so he had called Ram much earlier.

Ram was awake and reading his paper. All was well.

Sid reached his workplace and went into the chairman's office, where they both welcomed the credit head of Citibank Dubai. The group had applied to Citibank for a loan of USD 200 million for a plant expansion. As Sid finished his presentation and received a silent look of approval from the chairman, his cell phone rang. It was Ram from Mumbai. Sid excused himself and stepped out of the chairman's office into the corridor to take the call.

'I have had it with this temporary cook!' Ramparsad had taken a one-month leave of absence. 'He ruins my scrambled eggs every morning, and, can you believe it, he gives me biscuits with my morning tea! Doesn't he know that he should be doing that ONLY in the evening! I am going to sack him!' Ram was ranting. As Sid tried to reason with Ram, telling him that he was due in Mumbai the coming weekend and would sort everything out, the chairman stepped out of his office and joined Sid in the corridor. Placing his hand over the mouthpiece of the phone, Sid recounted to the chairman what his dad was ranting about.

The chairman, who was also over 70 years of age, said loudly, 'Your dad is absolutely correct, a satisfying morning meal is essential. Sack the cook.'

'We have left the credit head of Citibank, having applied for a massive loan, and these two old dudes are discussing scrambled eggs,' Sid thought wryly to himself. 'Good god, getting old must be fun.'

And the crowning glory of it all.

On one of the trips that Sid had made to Mumbai to check on Ram, he had noticed a picture of Lord Krishna hanging on the wall next to Ram's bed. Sid was taken aback. Whatever happened to Ram the staunch atheist, Ram the pragmatist, Ram the 'here and now' guy? Sid decided not to mention anything to Ram but leave it open for a later interesting discussion.

The next morning, when Sid opened his eyes, he witnessed a sight that he could have never ever imagined. He saw this old shrunken man, his father, bent over with folded hands, deep in prayer in front of a picture of Lord Krishna. Sid waited for Ram to finish and, when Ram turned, around Sid gesticulated with his hands as if to say, 'What is going on?'

Ram looked at his son with a sweet, shy smile and softly said, 'Just covering all the odds, beta.'

LET IT GO, DAD

Mahesh opened his eyes and stretched. The sunlight filtered in through the windows. It was early morning. A deep sense of well-being enveloped his consciousness. Today promised to be a great day, he thought to himself, as he looked at his wife Mina lovingly, fast asleep next to him.

Mina and Mahesh had met accidently at a club in Dubai about 10 years ago. Across the crowded room, pulsating with loud music, their eyes had locked in instant attraction that was apparent to all their friends. Mahesh had walked up to Mina and hesitantly started a conversation. Before you could blink, they had moved aside from their circle of friends and were deep in conversation. That was the start of an intimate, all-encompassing, soul-satisfying relationship. After that night, the two of them were virtually inseparable.

'We can talk non-stop, it's a relationship of complete communication,' they had both said, as they turned to each other to share every thought that flitted through their minds.

Before the first year was out, Mahesh and Mina were married in a joyous, love-filled ceremony. The first year was blissful and they were often complimented on how they were both glowing as their inner happiness shone through. They had discussed having children—they wanted to have only one child, and that too a girl child.

It was just a month after their first wedding anniversary, and Mina called Mahesh at work. 'You need to come home early, love, I am feeling a little bit under the weather,' she said. Mahesh cancelled his meetings for the day and rushed home. Mina opened the door with a shy smile, and, as Mahesh looked into her eyes, he just knew. With a whoop of joy, Mahesh enveloped her in a gentle hug. They both shed tears of happiness as they looked deeply into each other's eyes.

The rest of the pregnancy seemed to progress swiftly and, thankfully, quite uneventfully. Mina had cravings for ice cream at the most unexpected times of the day and night, so Mahesh learnt to stock the freezer with at least 12 varieties of ice cream.

In the sixth month of the pregnancy, Mina wanted to know the sex of the child so that she could plan the interior of the baby's room and select the clothes for the baby. The two of them went over to Dr Vikram's for a sonography. On hearing that the baby to come was a girl, the two of them let out whoops of sheer delight. All their wishes were being fulfilled. Dr Vikram had walked up to the two of them and hugged them together, quietly saying, 'In my 30 years of experience, this is the first time anybody has been so ecstatic at the announcement of a coming girl child. I bless you three from the bottom of my heart.'

Mika arrived with great fanfare. A beautiful, happy baby who would fall asleep at eight thirty p.m. after being fed and changed and would get up at five thirty a.m., giving her parents enough time to spend time together and to catch up on their sleep. They made a really good-looking threesome and were often complimented and blessed by random strangers when they stepped out.

A year later, Mahesh was offered an assignment in Muscat, Oman. It was a 'golden' offer that could just not be refused and the three of them, accompanied by Nirmala, their maid, who was devoted to Mika, soon found themselves comfortably settled into a large apartment in Muscat. With work challenges, settling into a new place, and making new friends, the years seemed to just fly past in a haze of contentment. Mahesh had been rewarded with promotions and bonuses in the ensuing years and was highly respected and appreciated by his employers.

Meena was very excited. She had planned a surprise party for Mahesh on his 40th birthday. Darius, Mahesh's best friend, would take Mahesh for a drink and then pretend to drop him home. Mahesh had been told by Mina that they would celebrate his birthday at Pavo Real, a quiet dinner for just the two of them, and Mahesh seemed to relish the idea. The party was a spectacular success, and, later that night, as the two of them undressed for bed, Mina turned and hugged Mahesh, saying, 'Honey, what gift can I give you to celebrate today?'

'What about a second child, a sibling for Mika so that she is never all alone?' Mahesh whispered.

Mina smiled and kissed Mahesh. 'Good idea, so let's get on with it,' she said.

Mina was pregnant within the month with their second child. Other than the morning nausea, which subsided after the first month of the pregnancy, everything seemed to be progressing well.

Mahesh glanced once more at Mina, fast asleep next to him, and once again thought to himself how beautiful she was in her pregnancy. Suddenly, he froze. He could hear a clear voice in his head. A young boy's voice: 'Dad, I am so sorry, it's not happening.' He knew instantly that it was his unborn child reaching out to him, and a feeling of dread and sadness enveloped his whole being. His rational mind told him that what he was experiencing was just not possible and that he should ignore the voice he had heard. However, he could not shake off the feeling of dread that lasted all the way until he reached his office and got busy with his work schedule. For the next three days, as soon as he opened his eyes every morning, he would clearly hear his unborn son's voice telling him he was sorry and that it was not happening. Mahesh would then be engulfed by an intense feeling of dread and loss that would only subside as the day progressed.

On the fourth day, he heard no voice.

A day later, Mina said to Mahesh, 'Let's take a break from the routine. Let's go to Dubai.' Mahesh had not told

Mina about his experience. Travelling to Dubai would entail a five-hour road trip. Was that feasible for a pregnant women, especially in the light of his experience?

Mahesh requested Mina to visit her gynaecologist before they planned their trip. The next morning, Mina visited the doctor, who called Mahesh and confirmed that everything was well with the baby and Mina and they were strong enough to take a five-hour road trip. Mahesh called his friends Rohan and Ramona to ask them if they could spend the weekend with them. Their friends were delighted and told Mahesh that they were to attend a dinner where he and Mina would get to meet their old Dubai acquaintances.

The road trip to Dubai went off without a hitch. Mika was strapped into a baby chair, the music was on, and Mina sat at the back with her feet up and her head cushioned by a pillow. Nirmala sat in front. Rohan hugged them warmly as Ramona grabbed Mika with a 'Give me my baby', and Mika and Ramona commenced the regular chatter that was the trademark of their relationship.

That night, Mika was kissed into bed by four adoring adults dressed for a night out, and Nirmala started her ritual bedtime story as the four stepped out. The party was great fun, and their friends were ever so happy to meet them. Mahesh was at the bar, regaling everybody with some spicy Muscat tales, when Ramona tapped him on his back and whispered into his ear, 'Mahesh, we need to leave soon, Mina is spotting, we need to get home asap.'

Mahesh excused himself and rushed to be with Mina. She was in no real discomfort, but spotting was not a good sign. As soon as they got home, Ramona helped Mina change into a loose nightie, made her lie down, and put her feet up by resting them on two fluffed-up pillows. Mina was soon asleep, and Ramona volunteered to sleep next to her.

'Please call me and let me know at the earliest sign of any change,' Mahesh requested Ramona, who just wordlessly hugged him.

Rohan fixed a stiff drink for Mahesh, who was deep in thought. 'Don't worry, man, all will be well, you will see. The spotting will stop on its own, just let everybody sleep it off,' Rohan said, trying to placate Mahesh. But Mahesh was recalling his experience with his unborn child and was extremely distressed. At that moment, he did not feel like sharing the experience with anybody, so he just kept silent.

After a very disturbed night, Mahesh rushed to Mina as soon as his eyes opened. The spotting had not stopped, Mina was in no pain, the situation remained unchanged. Mahesh then checked on Mika. Ramona and Nirmala had completed her morning ritual and Ramona was feeding Mika waffles and honey while the two of them kept up their regular chatter. It had been decided that they would consult the gynaecologist within the next one hour.

The gynaecologist kept it brief. 'I need to check her out. Please drive back today and be at the clinic at four p.m.,' she said. With that, Mahesh and his little family started the trip back to Muscat less than 48 hours after they had arrived in Dubai. Ramona and Rohan walked them to the car.

'Please let us know as soon as you are done at the doctor's,' Ramona said, kissing Mina and Mika goodbye and helping settle them both into the car.

As they drove away, Mahesh glanced in the rearview mirror and saw Ramona sobbing as Rohan reached out to hold her tight, his face in deep sorrow.

'They sense this is serious, just like I know,' Mahesh thought to himself.

It was as he feared. 'I am sorry, there is no heartbeat. We have lost the child,' the gynaecologist, Dr Sooriya, said with genuine sadness in her voice after examining Mina.

'What is the way forward now?' Mahesh asked 'Will you do a clean-up?'

'A clean up, or a DNC as it is better known, is not permitted in Oman. You will lose the foetus automatically, as the body rejects it. Given the circumstances, this is the best we can do. I am so sorry,' Dr Sooriya said.

Through all this, Mina was quiet and just looked worried and scared. Mahesh's primary concern was Mina's well-being. With a great feeling of loss and fear, the two of them headed home.

Both of them spoke to their parents in Mumbai, and it was decided that they would catch the first available flight to Mumbai. It was already seven p.m. in the evening. The first available flight to Mumbai was at ten thirty p.m.; tickets were available and could be bought at the airport. The bags were packed quickly and the four of them reached the airport at nine p.m. They just about managed to buy the tickets and board on time.

On the flight, Mina's spotting increased due to the air pressure. Mahesh had informed the airline crew as soon as they boarded about the situation, and they were very helpful. As soon as they disembarked, they were rushed through immigration and baggage claim into an ambulance. Mina's blood loss had increased dramatically. Mika, Nirmala, and the bags were managed by Mina's sister, who took them to her house and joined Mahesh and Mina in the hospital.

The DNC was done at eight a.m. in the morning. It was successful, and Mina was wheeled into a private room to recuperate. It was only then, when there were no fears for Mina's health, that the two allowed themselves to face their loss, and they sobbed into each other's arms. At that very moment, the doctor in the hospital stepped into the room and said, 'The last bit of information that I need to give you: the child was a boy.'

It was only then that Mahesh told Mina about their son reaching out to him. Mina only clutched Mahesh's arm and looked away.

It had been a very scary experience. Morning in Dubai, evening in Muscat, and night in Mumbai—24 hours of fear over Mina experiencing medical issues. She had fallen into a deep, exhausted sleep in the hospital. Her sister had arrived in the hospital to be with her, and Mahesh headed to the sister's house to make sure Mika was doing alright.

As Mahesh looked out of the car window at the Arabian Sea, all he could feel was an overpowering sense of sadness. His eyes filled with tears. Yes, they would come to terms with the loss of their son in time, but it would remain a lingering and deep emptiness in their souls.

Life went back to normal. Mahesh got a very good assignment in Dubai, and t he family moved there, much to the delight of Rohan and Ramona, who had been blessed with twins, two boys who kept them on their toes and adored Mika. Mika had blossomed into a young, intelligent teenager and left the family nest to study at Cambridge. She would come back home twice a year and she and the twins were inseparable when she was home.

It had been roughly 10 years since Mina's miscarriage. One night, Mahesh was in deep REM sleep. In his dream, he was following a young 10-year-old lad holding four multicoloured balloons in one hand. With the other hand, the boy was clasping his father's hand. Mahesh sensed a deep and abiding love between the father and son. In the distance was a small Indian village fair, a mela with a diminutive Ferris wheel, and the two of them seemed to be headed to it.

Mahesh knew in his heart that it was his unborn son that he was following. After he had been following them for what seemed a very long time, his son stopped, turned around, and looked lovingly into Mahesh's eyes.

'Dad, I am happy. Let it go, Dad. Please,' his son said. Then, turning around with a shy smile, he walked into the mela.

Mahesh sat up sweating, with a clear recollection of his dream and a strange sense of light-heartedness. It was as if the sadness and emptiness that he had carried within him all these years had been lifted.

'Till we meet again, my boy,' Mahesh said aloud into the night and lay down, falling into a peaceful sleep.

THE END GAME

Justin opened his eyes to the cacophony of birdsong outside his shuttered windows. It was another day. Sunlight streamed through the windows like a celestial benediction. He felt energised and at peace with the world. He stretched his limbs, got out of bed, and threw open the windows.

What a beautiful day it was. Blue skies, the sea breakers in the distance. A flock of parrots flew past just as a large kite swopped down to grab a tasty morsel from the pavement below. It was good to be alive, and Justin was just grateful that he could soak in this exquisite scenery.

Through 36 years of a fast-paced, highly driven life filled with intense workloads, excruciating deadlines, and post-work entertaining, stress had been Justin's constant companion. He was used to opening his eyes in the morning and having to plan his entire day to its minutest detail.

Things were different now. Justin had retired just a few months back and every day was open to infinite possibilities. At the same time, without any hobbies to fill up a significant part of his days, Justin was in a sense like a ship without a rudder. He felt blessed and happy every morning, but, as the day progressed, he would become clueless about how to spend his time.

Porthos, Justin's golden retriever, walked into the room, happy to see his companion awake, picked his leash up in his mouth, and walked up to Justin, dropping the leash at Justin's feet. 'Time for our walk, boss man.'

Justin hugged Porthos, who licked him good morning. Then Justin tied the leash around Porthos' neck and the two friends set out for their morning walk.

These walks with Porthos in the morning and at sunset, through the woods surrounding the house, had become the highlights of Justin's day. The trees were resplendent in wonderful hues of green and russet gold. The old gulmohar tree was in full bloom, heralding the onset of the monsoon. He watched a rabbit scurry into its burrow. Justin felt his spirit soar, and a deep contentment overcame his entire being.

'I am content,' Justin thought to himself, 'so why do I feel so empty inside? Is the rest of my life going to be this open-ended routine? Why can I not just enjoy myself?' Justin used these walks to reflect on what he wanted, nay, needed to do to feel good. The main issue, he had analysed, was that he wanted to feel relevant, but, sadly, he felt completely shunted to the backburner of life. Was that such a bad thing?

'Feeling relevant was not the only factor,' Justin thought to himself. 'The daily routine of going to work, interacting with people, and applying my mind to come up with business solutions managed to cover up the deep solitude that was my real life.'

Porthos came up and licked Justin's hand. 'Be at peace, boss man,' he seemed to say, sensing the disquiet in the air.

Justin had married Janice at the young age of 25. They had been complete opposites, and, after 25 years of a tempestuous relationship, Janice had left Justin and moved countries to be as far away from him as she could manage. Their acrimonious togetherness had resulted in one child, Greg, who blamed the two of them for a miserable childhood spent watching the two people he venerated and adored the most destroy each other emotionally. At 30, Greg did not want anything to do with either of his parents, so he did not call, did not keep in touch, and did not participate in their lives.

Justin was truly all by himself, physically and emotionally.

Justin decided to dial his sister Racheal. Racheal lived in a senior citizen retirement home on the outskirts of the city. She was 10 years older than Justin and had literally mothered Justin when he was a young lad. She was a widow, and her children had settled overseas. Although she, too, was all by herself, Racheal had managed to create a busy, well connected routine that seemed to keep her satisfied and fulfilled.

'Hi sis, wazzup!' Justin bellowed into the phone, as Racheal was now hard of hearing. Racheal ran through her daily routine with Justin. The buffet breakfast in the dining room had consisted of cereal and she had ordered a side plate of fried eggs. She was getting ready to go watch

Butch Cassidy and the Sundance Kid in the auditorium with the other 50 residents of the retirement home, after which it would be time for lunch and then a refreshing afternoon siesta. She and her friends would meet in the evening on the patio outside the dining room at about five p.m., then go into the dining room for dinner at seven p.m. She would be back in her apartment by eight p.m., after which she would watch the news on the box until ten thirty before turning in for the night. Her son Ralph would be calling today, so she was looking forward to hearing the gossip about her grandchildren.

'Very good, sis. Take care, talk to you soon,' Justin said, signing off, and then muttered to himself, 'Why cannot I be as fulfilled with a routine as Racheal is?'

Porthos and Justin headed home. Just as they reached the front door, Justin heard the landline ringing impatiently. He struggled to open the door and dashed to the phone console to answer it. It was Ronaldo, his colleague from his last workplace, who had retired on the same day as Justin.

'Justin, ole chap, what ho,' Ronaldo boomed warmly. 'How are you doing, my friend?'

Justin assured Ronaldo that all was well with him and that everything was running smoothly and routinely.

'Nothing is routine with me, Justin, I am just having a whale of a time. Do you remember my trepidation about how I was going to fill up the emptiness of my retirement? Well, I just don't have the time to breathe.

I have started mentoring young adults in the corporate world to help them achieve their goals. I have about 15 clients and they keep me actively engaged. So, not only do I have an insanely busy day but I am also contributing to the development of individuals and making some serious money,' Ronaldo enthused.

Justin was happy for Ronaldo. 'Let's catch up for a drink next week,' he suggested, 'and you can regale me with your individual cases.' They agreed to meet the next week at their old after-hours bar, Geoffrey's.

Justin felt a twinge of envy. 'I definitely do not want to be as engaged with assignments as Ronaldo seems to be,' he thought to himself, 'but at least Ronaldo has defined a path for himself, lucky chap.'

It was time for a shower and some freshening up, and Justin was looking forward to the steam room and sauna treatment that would precede the shower today. As he headed to his room, he paused to look back at his drawing room. Two years ago, in anticipation of and preparation for his retirement, Justin had invested a sizeable amount of his savings in refurbishing his house. The style was contemporary-classic. His house was not only tastefully done, with great attention to detail—Justin had even selected sofa fabrics, curtains, etc., personally—but was also very utilitarian, with all the comforts of modern day life. The master bedroom opened into a fully equipped gymnasium with a steam room, a sauna, and a jacuzzi—the full spa treatment. The net effect, with the

Persian carpets, crystal chandeliers, brass flowerpots, and priceless paintings, was understated elegance and luxury. In his typical assertive manner, and relying entirely on his own aesthetic taste, without any input from a designer, Justin had created the home of his dreams.

'I love this house,' he thought and, smiling to himself, entered his bedroom. He soaked in the jacuzzi and savoured the feeling of well-being. 'What will today bring,' he pondered. 'Maybe it's all about living in the moment, enjoying every second of just being alive. Balderdash, bah. That's easier said than done. I definitely need my life to be more exciting than that. I am not ready for the sadhu way of life as yet. I need more.'

Justin glanced at the wall clock; it was nearly noon. He had a one p.m. lunch date at the country club with his college mate Sherry. 'Must hurry up,' he said aloud to himself. After all, it was a 45-minute drive to the club. Justin was a simple dresser—denim jeans and a tucked-in pastel-coloured long-sleeved shirt and loafers was his standard outfit. Today, he decided to give it a twist. He selected tan trousers, a brown and black checked shirt, chino loafers, and the piece de resistance—a Panama hat. He looked at himself in the mirror and thought, 'You smart devil, you,' then picked up the car keys from the Lladro bowl near the door and headed towards the Mercedes.

As he drove through the crowded roads of the city, Justin's thoughts turned to Sherry. He had dated Sherry for four years through their undergraduate years at

Northwestern. Sherry then moved on to Columbia University to do her Master's in communication whilst Justin took up a job in Chicago. As is often said, absence makes the heart wander instead of growing fonder. Sherry met John at Columbia, married John, made a home in New York, had two children, Jean and Samantha, now married with children of their own, and, suddenly, late last winter, became a widow. John had collapsed at work with a massive stroke.

Justin had rushed to be with Sherry. They had over the years become very good friends in the true sense of the word. They both felt understood, accepted, and very comfortable in each other's presence, and had both decided that the friendship was far more important than any rekindling of a romantic liaison.

Justin entered the lunch room at the club and was ushered to a table for two. Sherry was already seated at the table, looking lovely and svelte. She had aged very well. She wore her years with elegance and panache, and her eyes lit up at the sight of Justin.

'Ooh la la,' Sherry gushed, 'someone is looking very fancy today.'

Justin threw his head back and laughed and reparteed with a 'You look lovely, my dear, as always.'

The server walked over, and they placed their orders for lunch: Atlantic cod with a French Sauvignon blanc. Sherry had just returned from a 14-day Mediterranean cruise. She had had such a good time on the ship that she had decided she would travel for at least four months in the year, including at least two cruises.

'It makes life so very exciting, Justin. You get to make new friends, you get to see new places, you get to experience new lifestyles. You must try it sometime, Justin, it will add flavour to your life,' Sherry said excitedly. 'In fact, the club is organising a group of 20 senior citizens for a Nile cruise. Should I register both our names?'

'Let me think about it, my dear,' Justin responded.

Lunch was fun. Good food, good wine, great company; they spoke about Sherry's kids and grandkids, the new friends she had made, and her current passion for quilt-making. Justin updated her on what he had been thinking about lately. How, although he was content and felt good about himself, his day at times felt like a void that he needed to fill up.

Sherry's advice was, 'Honey, no one can tell you what is the right formula for you. You will have to struggle through these days and define your path going forward for yourself. If you need someone to talk to anytime of the day or night, call me. I will always have your back.'

After a satisfying lunch, Justin escorted Sherry to her car. She hugged him warmly and then, with a quick wave of her hand, she was gone.

As Justin started up his car to head home, he thought to himself, 'I am truly blessed to have such devoted friends like Sherry. But travelling and seeing new places is not my forte. I dislike the process of adjusting to a change in scenery. I like familiar things around me. And, good God, the thought of being trapped in a huge boat with over 5,000 beings and no land in sight—like Noah—fills me with dread. I like the sanctuary of my own home. And, as for travelling four months in a year, NEVER.' He shuddered.

Porthos barked excitedly as Justin walked into the house. After a bout of licking and rapid tail-wagging, Porthos headed back for his afternoon nap. Justin checked Porthos' food bowl; it had been wiped clean. Both Justin and Porthos stretched out on their beds for their afternoon siesta.

Justin got up with a start. Someone had rung the doorbell. It was five p.m.

'Oh yes, this must be David,' Justin remembered. Although David lived in the house next to Justin's and had been his neighbour for 10 years, they were just nodding acquaintances. Justin quickly brushed back his hair and walked to the main door. He welcomed David in and apologised for having taken time to open the door; David on his part apologised for encroaching on Justin's siesta time.

Justin fixed a cup of coffee for David and himself and settled down in the imperial chair to listen to what David had to say. David had been running a shelter for the homeless in the City Centre Area. The work was escalating, with the increasing number of homeless persons needing supplies and medical attention, so David was looking for volunteers. He had heard that Justin had retired and wanted to know if Justin would like to volunteer. He would be required to be at the shelter three days every week, from nine a.m. to one p.m.

Justin was taken aback for a minute. Without appearing to be completely self-serving and self-centred, how could he possibly tell David that helping others was of no interest to him? It really did not have any effect on his well-being. Justin excused himself from the proposed assignment with a lie: 'David, I would love to help out, but, although I have retired, I am a consultant with my earlier employer and I work full workdays from home, so I am afraid I cannot volunteer. I am so sorry.'

David looked disappointed and left for the shelter.

'So what does that make me?' Justin asked Porthos. 'Not a very nice person, I guess, but I am being honest. Let's go for our evening walk, mon ami.'

As the two of them entered the forest, Justin analysed his feelings. Strangely, he was not ashamed of himself for not wanting to help others. He just thought, 'Well, this is me.'

Back from their walk, Justin looked up at the grandfather clock in the hallway. It was seven p.m. Hakim, Justin's old friend from Dubai, was coming over for dinner. Hakim was an oncologist and a widower with no children. His wife Fatima had been very fond of Justin and had been Justin's confidante. She had been a rock of support for Justin when his marriage to Janice had fallen apart and had tirelessly, without any success, tried to counsel both of them to make the marriage work; but, in the end, nothing on the planet could bridge their essential differences. Fatima had been a wise, compassionate, and caring friend and wife, and, after her passing, Hakim, always a very quiet person, retreated further into a life of solitude and service.

Justin changed quickly and ordered in from Farsi, the Persian restaurant. Hakim liked tahini with mutton kebabs accompanied with red wine sangria. Dessert would be tiramisu, a goblet of Hennessy XO, and a cigar. Justin bustled around in the kitchen getting everything in place whilst Porthos watched the goings-on comfortably from the kitchen door.

When Porthos stood up, wagging his tail, Justin knew that Hakim was at the door. As he was walking to the door, the doorbell rang; Justin threw open the door and enveloped Hakim in a bear hug. The friends settled themselves in, both of them comfortable in their favourite positions in the living room, Hakim in the lazy boy, Justin at one end of the leather sofa with his legs stretched out on it, and Porthos, having given Hakim a resounding welcome lick, settled at Justin's feet.

Hakim, in his inimitable style, charged into the core of the issue. 'What are you disturbed about, my friend?' he asked Justin. 'I sensed you are restless within when you hugged me. Talk to me.'

Justin explained the confusion he was feeling, trying to express what he was going through. 'I am content, yet I feel empty,' he concluded.

Hakim looked fondly at his friend and reflected on what Justin had just told him. In his experience as an oncologist, Hakim had come close to understanding the meaning of life. The joy of experiencing it and the dread of watching it slip away. When you were faced with a terminal cancer patient who had just six months to live, what on earth could you say to that person? He remembered when he first read Fatima's test readings. She had fourth-stage cervical cancer. According to his estimate, Fatima would not be able to live for more than four months. What would he tell her? She had a right to know. How would he handle the abyss he felt had opened up below him? 'Continue living without Fatima? How is that even humanly possible?' he had thought to himself.

At that very moment, Fatima had walked into the room. She had looked at him and then walked into his arms and hugged him. 'How much time?' she had asked.

He had started ranting about how they would fight and overcome the cancer and how everything would work out just right in the end. She had put a finger to his lips and just kissed him. He had broken down sobbing and she had just held him and stroked his head.

Fatima had taught Hakim what living was all about. In the last four months of her life, she taught him to get up every morning and marvel at the beauty of nature, she taught him to meditate for an hour a day and go inwards to find the core of peace and silence within him, and, above all, she taught him to accept the cycles of life. When the time came, she called him to her bedside and whispered, 'All things must pass, my love, enjoy the journey and savour the moment.'

Today, a year later after Fatima's death, Hakim had managed to find that sea of silence within himself and felt truly self-actualised and complete.

'Justin, I think it is time for you to delve inward into discovering the sea of equanimity that is at the core of each of us,' Hakim said to his friend. 'You have experienced the outward journey and apparently have been fulfilled by that. This is the next logical stage. You need to start yoga and meditation. My guru Ravishanker can help you realise your path, provided he feels you are a true seeker. Give it a thought, my friend.' And, as if to drive home the point he was making, he ended by saying, 'This is the advice my Fatima would have given you. Now let's eat.'

Dinner was delicious. The food was perfect. The initial conversation was about the latest nanotechnological developments. Justin was fascinated to hear that future heart surgeries could be conducted without having to carry out an open-heart surgery. Justin had some experience with AI and updated Hakim on the latest trends. Before they knew it, it was time to call it a night.

'Thank you for a wonderful evening, Justin,' Hakim said as they walked to Hakim's car, and added, 'Think about what I just said and let me know if I should get Ravishanker to come and see you.' They hugged each other good night, and Hakim drove away.

Justin settled into bed while Porthos settled at Justin's feet. Within 10 minutes, both friends were in deep REM sleep.

Justin sat up in bed with a start. He suddenly had an epiphany that seemed to coalesce all the thoughts raging within him. Porthos lazily opened one eye and gave him a quizzical look.

What was the protocol for the endgame? After all the worldly responsibilities were done with, how was one supposed to play out the closing journey? The four stages of life in the dharma concept of Hinduism—brahmacharya or student, grihasta or householder, vanaprastha or retired, and sannyasa or renunciate—had defined the journey of life, according to age-old wisdom.

'Maybe I am at stage three,' Justin thought. 'Will I ever get to stage four? I doubt it. But I can for sure focus on stage three. That is the way ahead. But how does one perfect stage three? What do I need to do?'

Justin realised that the answer was, in the truest sense, very simple. The endgame had to be experienced with joy and gratitude. The key tools to getting there were self-discipline, a routine, and the inward journey through meditation and yoga. Justin decided to call Hakim in the morning and ask for a meeting with Ravishanker.

With a sense of purpose, Justin settled down to go back to sleep as Porthos gave a deep sigh, glad that the night's disturbance had subsided.

The sunlight streamed through the shuttered window. Justin opened his eyes. He stretched his limbs. The endgame protocol was detailed clearly before him like a path laid out for him to follow. He felt content and strangely relevant. He realised that he was relevant to himself and that was more than enough. His goal going forward was self-actualisation and, as he bounded out of bed to welcome the new day and kissed Porthos good morning, there was no void inside of him to fill up.

www.ingramcontent.com/pod-product-compliance
Lightning Source LLC
LaVergne TN
LVHW091112150826
845673LV00002B/787

* 9 7 9 8 8 9 1 3 3 9 9 8 9 *